"You Are Obnoxious And Uptight At Times. Other Times…"

She circled a hand in the air, trying to pluck out one or two of his less irritating traits. "Other times you surprise me, Mr. Ambassador. Like tonight, for instance, when you got behind the bar. You went above and beyond the call of duty there."

"I'm a man of many talents," he said smugly. "And that reminds me. I was promised payment for services rendered."

"So you were. Have you given any thought to what form that payment should take?"

"Oh, sweetheart, I haven't thought of anything else all evening."

Red flags went up instantly. Gina knew she was playing with fire. Knew the last thing she should do was slide her feet off his lap and curl them under her, rising to her knees in the process.

All she had to do was look at him….

* * *

The Diplomat's Pregnant Bride
is part of the Duchess Diaries duet:
Two royal granddaughters
on their way to happily ever after!

* * *

If you're on Twitter,
tell us what you think of Harlequin Desire!
#harlequindesire

Dear Reader,

When my niece Cori gave her mom and me a private, behind-the-scenes tour of where she worked, I could sense immediately how many great stories lay behind the different events hosted at Clayton on the Park. I thought then what fun it would be to craft a book that included the exciting business hosting events that mark such major milestones in people's lives.

And I had the perfect heroine in Gina St. Sebastian, who loves nothing more than a good party! Or did, until life suddenly caught up with her.

I hope you enjoy Gina and Jack's story, and will watch for more books featuring the sizzling St. Sebastians in the near future.

All my best,

Merline

THE DIPLOMAT'S PREGNANT BRIDE

—

MERLINE LOVELACE

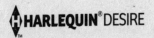

Recycling programs
for this product may
not exist in your area.

ISBN-13: 978-0-373-73287-6

THE DIPLOMAT'S PREGNANT BRIDE

Copyright © 2013 by Merline Lovelace

Printed in U.S.A.

www.Harlequin.com

MERLINE LOVELACE

A career Air Force officer, Merline Lovelace served at bases all over the world. When she hung up her uniform for the last time she decided to combine her love of adventure with a flair for storytelling, basing many of her tales on her own experiences in uniform. Since then she's produced more than ninety action-packed sizzlers, many of which have made the USA TODAY and Waldenbooks bestseller lists. Over eleven million copies of her books are available in some thirty countries.

When she's not tied to her keyboard, Merline enjoys reading, chasing little white balls around the fairways of Oklahoma and traveling to new and exotic locales with her handsome husband, Al. Check her website at www.merlinelovelace.com or friend her on Facebook for news and information about her latest releases.

To my gorgeous niece Cori and Jane and the rest of the crew at Clayton on the Park, in Scottsdale. Thanks for the inside look at the ups and downs of an event coordinator's life!

Prologue

I could not have asked for two more beautiful or loving granddaughters. From the first day they came to live with me—one so young and frightened, the other still in diapers—they filled the empty spaces in my heart with light and joy. Now Sarah, my quiet, elegant Sarah, is about to marry her handsome Dev. The wedding takes place in a few hours, and I ache with happiness for her.

And with such worry for her sister. My darling Eugenia has waltzed through life, brightening even the sourest dispositions with her sparkling smile and carefree, careless joie de vivre. Now, quite suddenly that carelessness has caught up with her. She's come face-to-face with reality, and I can only pray the strength and spirit I know she possesses will help her through the difficult days ahead.

Enough of this. I must dress for the wedding. Then it's off to the Plaza, which has been the scene of so many significant events in my life. But none to match the delight of this one!

From the diary of Charlotte,
Grand Duchess of Karlenburgh

One

Gina St. Sebastian forced a smile to hide her gritted teeth. "Good Lord, you're stubborn, Jack."

"*I'm* stubborn?"

The irate male standing before her snapped his sun-bleached brows together. Ambassador John Harris Mason III was tanned, tawny-haired and a trim, athletic six-one. He was also used to being in charge. The fact that he couldn't control Gina or the situation they now found themselves in irritated him no end.

"You're pregnant with my child, dammit. Yet you refuse to even discuss marriage."

"Oh, for...! Trumpet the news to the whole world, why don't you?"

Scowling, Gina craned her neck to peer around the bank of gardenias shielding her and Jack from the other guests in the Terrace Room of New York City's venerable Plaza Hotel. With its exquisitely restored Italian Renaissance ceiling and crystal chandeliers modeled after those in the Palace of Versailles, it made a fabulous venue for a wedding.

A wedding put together on extremely short notice! They'd had less than two weeks to pull it off. The groom's billions had eased the time crunch considerably, as had the miracle worker Dev Hunter employed as his executive assistant. Gina had done all the planning, though, and she would not allow the man she'd spent one wild weekend with to disrupt her sister's wedding day.

Luckily no one seemed to have heard his caustic comment. The band was currently pulsing out the last bars of a lively merengue. Sarah and Dev were on the dance floor, along with the St. Sebastians' longtime housekeeper, Maria, and most of the guests invited to the elegant affair.

Gina's glance shot from the dancers to the lace-clad woman sitting ramrod-straight in her chair, hands crossed on the ebony head of her cane. The duchess was out of earshot, too, thank God! Hearing her younger granddaughter's pregnancy broadcast to the world at large wouldn't have fit with her notions of proper behavior.

Relieved, Gina swung back to Jack. "I won't have you spoil my sister's wedding with another argument. Please lower your voice."

He took the hint and cranked down the decibels, if not his temper. "We haven't had ten minutes alone to talk about this since you got back from Switzerland."

As if she needed the reminder! She'd flown to Switzerland exactly one day after she'd peed on a purple stick and felt her world come crashing down around her. She'd had to get away from L.A., had to breathe in the sharp, clean air of the snow-capped Alps surrounding Lake Lucerne while trying to decide what to do. After a day and a night of painful soul-searching, she'd walked into one of Lucerne's ultramodern clinics. Ten minutes later, she'd turned around and walked out again. But not before making two near-hysterical calls. The first was to Sarah—her sister, her protector, her dearest friend. The second, unfortunately, was to the handsome, charismatic and thoroughly annoying diplomat now confronting her.

By the time Sarah had made the frantic dash from Paris in response to her sister's call, Gina's jagged nerves had smoothed a little. Her hard-won poise shattered once again, however, when Jack Mason showed up on the scene. She hadn't expected him to jump a plane, much less express such fierce satisfaction over her decision to have their child.

Actually, the decision had surprised Gina as much as it had Jack. She was the flighty, irresponsible sister. The good-time girl, always up for a weekend skiing in Biarritz or a sail through the blue-green waters of the Caribbean. Raised by their grandmother, she and Sarah had been given the education and sophisticated lifestyle the duchess insisted was their birthright. Only recently had the sisters learned how deeply Grandmama had gone into debt to provide that lifestyle. Since then, Gina had made a determined effort to support herself. A good number of efforts, actually. Sadly, none of the careers she'd dabbled in had held her mercurial interest for very long.

Modeling had turned out to be a drag. All those hot lights and temperamental photographers snapping orders like constipated drill sergeants. Escorting small, select tour groups to the dazzling capitals of Europe was even more of a bore. How in the world could she have imagined she'd want to make a career of chasing down lost luggage or shuffling room assignments to placate a whiny guest who didn't like the view in hers?

Gina had even tried to translate her brief sojourn at Italy's famed cooking school, the Academia Barilla, into a career as a catering chef. That misguided attempt had barely lasted a week. But when her exasperated boss booted her out of the kitchen and into the front office, she'd discovered her apparently one real talent. She was far better at planning parties than cooking for them. Especially when clients walked in waving a checkbook and orders to pull out all the stops for their big event.

She was so good, in fact, that she intended to support herself and her child by coordinating soirees for the rich and famous. But first she had to convince her baby's father that she neither needed nor wanted the loveless marriage he was offering.

"I appreciate your concern, Jack, but…"

"Concern?"

The handsome, charismatic ambassador kept his voice down as she'd requested, but looked as though he wanted let loose with both barrels. His shoulders were taut under his hand-tailored tux. Below his neatly trimmed caramel-colored hair, his brown eyes drilled into her.

Gina couldn't help but remember how those eyes had snared hers across a crowded conference room six weeks ago and signaled instant, electric attraction. How his oh-so-skilled mouth had plundered her throat and her breasts and her belly. How…

Oh, for pity's sake! Why remember the heat that had sizzled so hot and fast between them? That spontaneous combustion wouldn't happen again. Not now. Not with everything else that was going on in their lives.

"But," she continued with a forced smile, "you have to agree a wedding reception is hardly the time or place for a discussion like this."

"Name the time," he challenged. "And the place."

"All right! Tomorrow. Twelve noon." Cornered, she named the first place she could think of. "The Boathouse in Central Park."

"I'll be there."

"Fine. We'll get a table in a quiet corner and discuss this like the mature adults we are."

"Like the mature adult at least one of us is."

Gina hid a wince. The biting sarcasm stung, but she had to admit it wasn't far off the mark. The truth was she'd pretty much flitted through life, laughing at its absurdities, always counting on Sarah or Grandmama to bail her out of trouble every time she tumbled into it. All that changed about ten minutes after she peed on that damned stick. Her flitting days were over. It was time to take responsibility for herself and her baby.

Which she would.

She would!

"I'll see you tomorrow."

Chin high, she swept around the bank of gardenias.

Jack let her go. She was right. This wasn't the time or the place to hammer some sense into her. Not that he held much hope his calm, rational arguments would penetrate that thick mane of silvery blond curls or spark a glimmer of understanding in those baby-doll blue eyes.

He'd now spent a total of five days—one long, wild weekend and two frustrating days in Switzerland—in Gina St. Sebastian's company. More than enough time to confirm the woman constituted a walking, talking bundle of contradictions. She was jaw-droppingly gorgeous and so sensual she made grown men go weak at the knees, but also friendly and playful as a kitten. Well-educated, yet in many ways naive beyond belief. And almost completely oblivious to the world around her unless it directly impacted her, her sister or her dragon lady of a grandmother.

Pretty much his exact opposite, Jack thought grimly as he tracked her progress across the crowded room. He came from a long line of coolheaded, clear-thinking Virginians who believed their vast wealth brought with it equally great responsibility. Jack's father and grandfather had served as advisors to presidents in times of national crisis. He himself had served in several diplomatic posts before being appointed the State Department's ambassador-at-large for counterterrorism at the ripe old age of thirty-two. As such, he'd traveled to some of the most volatile, violent trouble spots in the world. Recently he'd returned to State Department headquarters in Washington, D.C., to translate his hard-won field knowledge into policies and procedures that would improve the security of U.S. diplomatic personnel around the world.

His job demanded long days and long nights. Stress rode on his shoulders like hundred-pound weights. Yet he couldn't remember any issue, any recalcitrant bureaucrat or political pundit, who frustrated him as much as Gina St. Sebastian. She was pregnant with his child, dammit! The child he was determined would carry his name.

The child he and Catherine had tried so hard to have.

The familiar pain knifed into him. The feeling wasn't as vicious as it had once been, but was still ferocious enough to carve up his insides. The lively conversation around him faded. The flower-bedecked room blurred. He could almost see her, almost hear her Boston Brahman accent. Catherine—brilliant, politically savvy Catherine—would have grasped the irony in his present situation at once. She would have...

"You look like you could use a drink, Mason."

With an immense effort of will, Jack blanked the memory of his dead wife and turned to the new groom. Dev Hunter held a crystal tumbler in one hand and offered one to Jack with the other.

"Scotch, straight up," he said dryly. "I saw you talking to Gina and figured you could use it."

"You figured right."

Jack took the tumbler and tipped it toward the man who might soon become his brother-in-law. Not might, he amended grimly as they clinked glasses, would.

"To the St. Sebastian sisters," Hunter said, his gaze shifting to the two women standing with their heads together across the room. "It took some convincing, but I got mine to the altar. Good luck getting yours there."

The Scotch went down with a well-mannered bite. Jack savored its smoky tang and eyed the sisters. They were a study in contrasts. Dark-haired Sarah was impossibly elegant in a clinging ivory gown with feathered clasps at each shoulder and glowed with the incandescent beauty of a bride. Blonde, bubbly Gina was barely six weeks pregnant and showed no signs of a baby bump. She was still slender but more generously endowed than her sister. Her flame-colored, body-hugging, strapless and backless sheath outlined her seductive curves to perfection.

Jack's fingers tightened on the tumbler. Six weeks after the fact and he could still remember how he'd positioned those seductive hips under his. How he'd buried his hands in her silky hair and lost himself in that lush body and those laughing blue eyes.

They'd used protection that weekend. Went through a whole damned box of it, as he recalled. So much for playing the odds.

"I'll get her to the altar," he vowed. "One way or another."

Hunter raised a brow but refrained from comment as his bride smiled and crooked a finger. "I'm being summoned. I'll talk to you again when Sarah and I get back from our honeymoon."

He handed his empty tumbler to a passing waiter and started for his wife, then turned back. "Just for the record, Mason, my money's on Gina. She's got more of the duchess in her than she realizes. And speaking of the duchess..."

Jack followed his glance and saw the silver-haired St. Sebastian matriarch thumping her way toward them. A long-sleeve, high-necked dress of ecru lace draped her slight frame. A trio of rings decorated her arthritic fingers. Leaning heavily on her cane with her left hand, Charlotte dismissed her new grandson-in-law with an imperious wave of the right.

"Gina says it's time for you and Sarah to change out of your wedding finery. You only have an hour to get to the airport."

"It's my plane, Charlotte. I don't think it'll leave without us."

"I should hope not." Her ringed fingers flapped again. "Do go away, Devon. I want to talk to Ambassador Mason."

Jack didn't consciously go into a brace but he could feel

his shoulders squaring as he faced Gina's diminutive, indomitable grandmother.

He knew all about her. He should. He'd dug up the file the State Department had compiled on Charlotte St. Sebastian, once Grand Duchess of the tiny principality of Karlenburgh, when she fled her Communist-overrun country more than five decades ago. After being forced to witness her husband's brutal execution, she'd escaped with the clothes on her back, her infant daughter in her arms and a fortune in jewels hidden inside the baby's teddy bear.

She'd eventually settled in New York City and become an icon of the social and literary scenes. Few of the duchess's wealthy, erudite friends were aware this stiff-spined aristocrat had pawned her jewels over the years to support herself and the two young granddaughters who'd come to live with her after the tragic death of their parents. Jack knew only because Dev Hunter had hinted that he should tread carefully where Charlotte and her granddaughters' financial situation were concerned.

Very carefully. Jack's one previous encounter with the duchess made it clear her reduced circumstances had not diminished either her haughty air or the fierce protectiveness she exhibited toward her granddaughters. That protectiveness blazed in her face now.

"I just spoke with Gina. She says you're still trying to convince her to marry you."

"Yes, I am."

"Why?"

Jack was tempted to fall back on Gina's excuse and suggest that a wedding reception was hardly the proper place for this discussion. The steely look in the duchess's faded blue eyes killed that craven impulse.

"I think the reason would be obvious, ma'am. Your granddaughter's carrying my child. I want to give her and the baby the protection of my name."

The reply came coated with ice. "The St. Sebastian name

provides more than enough cachet for my granddaughter and her child."

Well, hell! And he called himself a diplomat! Jack was delivering a mental swift kick when the duchess raised her cane and jabbed the tip into his starched shirt front.

"Tell me one thing, Mr. Ambassador. Do you honestly believe the baby is yours?"

He didn't hesitate. "Yes, ma'am, I do."

The cane took another sharp jab at his sternum.

"Why?"

For two reasons, one of which Jack wasn't about to share. He was still pissed that his father had reacted to the news that he would be a grandfather by hiring a private investigator. With ruthless efficiency the P.I. had dug into every nook and cranny of Gina St. Sebastian's life for the past three months. The report he submitted painted a portrait of a woman who bounced from job to job and man to man with seeming insouciance. Yet despite his best efforts, the detective hadn't been able to turn up a single lover in Gina's recent past except John Harris Mason III.

Furious, Jack had informed his father that he didn't need any damned report. He'd known the baby was his from the moment Gina called from Switzerland, sobbing and nearly incoherent. He now tried to convey that same conviction to the ferocious woman about to skewer him with her cane.

"As I've discovered in our brief time together, Duchess, your granddaughter has her share of faults. So do I. Neither of us have tried to deceive the other about those faults, however."

"What you mean," she countered with withering scorn, "is that neither of you made any protestations of eternal love or devotion before you jumped into bed together."

Jack refused to look away, but damned if he didn't feel heat crawling up the back of his neck. Wisely, he sidestepped the jumping-into-bed issue. "I'll admit I have a lot to learn yet about your granddaughter but my sense is she doesn't lie. At least not about something this important," he added with more frankness than tact.

To his relief, the duchess lowered the cane and leaned on it with both hands. "You're correct in that assessment. Gina doesn't lie."

She hesitated, and a look that combined both pride and exasperation crossed her aristocratic features. "If anything, the girl is too honest. She tends to let her feelings just pour out, along with whatever she happens to be thinking at the time."

"So I noticed," Jack said, straight-faced.

Actually, Gina's exuberance and utter lack of pretense had delighted him almost as much as her luscious body during their weekend together. Looking back, Jack could admit he'd shucked a half-dozen layers of his sober, responsible self during that brief interlude. They hadn't stayed shucked, of course. Once he'd returned to Washington, he'd been engulfed in one crisis after another. Right up until that call from Switzerland.

The duchess reclaimed his attention with a regal toss of her head. "I will say this once, young man, and I suggest you take heed. My granddaughter's happiness is my first—my *only*—concern. Whatever Eugenia decides regarding you and the baby, she has my complete support."

"I wouldn't expect anything less, ma'am."

"Hrrrmph." She studied him with pursed lips for a moment before delivering an abrupt non sequitur. "I knew your grandfather."

"You did?"

"He was a member of President Kennedy's cabinet at the time. Rather stiff and pompous, as I recall."

Jack had to grin. "That sounds like him."

"I invited him and your grandmother to a reception I hosted for the Sultan of Oman right here, in these very rooms. The Kennedys attended. So did the Rockefellers."

A distant look came into her eyes. A smile hovered at the corners of her mouth.

"I wore my pearls," she murmured, as much to herself as to her listener. "They roped around my neck three times before draping almost to my waist. Jackie was quite envious."

He bet she was. Watching the duchess's face, listening to her cultured speech with its faint trace of an accent, Jack nursed the hope that marriage to her younger granddaughter might not be such a disaster, after all.

With time and a little guidance on his part, Gina could learn to curb some of her impulsiveness. Maybe even learn to think before she blurted out whatever came into her mind. Not that he wanted to dim her sparkling personality. Just rein it in a bit so she'd feel comfortable in the restrained diplomatic circles she'd be marrying into.

Then, of course, there was the sex.

Jack kept his expression politely attentive. His diplomatic training and years of field experience wouldn't allow him to do otherwise. Yet every muscle in his body went taut as all-too-vivid images from his weekend with Gina once again grabbed him.

He hadn't been a saint since his wife died, but neither had he tomcatted around. Five women in six years didn't exactly constitute a world record. Yet the hours he'd spent in that Beverly Hills penthouse suite with Gina St. Sebastian made him come alive in ways he hadn't felt since…

Since Catherine.

Shaking off the twinge of guilt that thought brought, Jack addressed the woman just coming out of her reverie of presidents and pearls.

"Please believe me, Duchess. I want very much to do right by both your granddaughter and our child."

Those shrewd, pale eyes measured him for long, uncomfortable moments. Jack had faced cold-blooded dictators whose stares didn't slice anywhere as close to the bone as this white-haired, seemingly frail woman's did.

"You may as well call me Charlotte," she said finally. "I

suspect we may be seeing a good deal of each other in the weeks ahead."

"I suspect we may."

"Now, if you'll excuse me, I must help Sarah prepare to depart for her honeymoon."

Two

After Sarah changed and left for the airport with Dev, Gina escorted her grandmother and Maria down to the limo she'd ordered for them.

"I'll be a while," she warned as the elevator opened onto the Plaza's elegant lobby. "I want to make sure Dev's family is set for their trip home tomorrow."

"I should think that clever, clever man Dev employs as his executive assistant has the family's travel arrangements well in hand."

"He does. He's also going to take care of shipping the wedding gifts back to L.A., thank goodness. But I need to verify the final head count and see he has a complete list of the bills to expect."

The duchess stiffened, and Gina gave herself a swift mental kick. Dang it! She shouldn't have mentioned those bills. As she and Sarah knew all too well, covering the cost of the wedding had come dangerously close to a major point of contention between Dev and the duchess. Charlotte had insisted on taking care of the expenses traditionally paid by the bride's family. It was a real tribute to Dev's negotiating skills that he and Grandmama had reached an agreement that didn't totally destroy her pride.

And now Gina had to bring up the sensitive subject again! It was Jack's fault, she thought in disgust. Their confrontation had thrown her off stride. Was still throwing her off. Why the heck had she agreed to meet him for lunch tomorrow?

She was still trying to figure that one out when the limo pulled up to the Plaza's stately front entrance. The driver got out to open the door but before his two passengers slid into the backseat, the duchess issued a stern warning.

"Don't overtax yourself, Eugenia. Pregnancy saps a woman's strength, especially during the first few months. You'll find you're more fatigued than usual."

"Fatigue hasn't been a problem yet. Or morning sickness, knock on…"

She glanced around for some wood to rap. She settled for wiggling a branch of one of the massive topiary trees guarding the front entrance.

"My breasts are swollen up like water balloons, though. And my nipples ache like you wouldn't believe." Grimacing, she rolled her shoulders to ease the constriction of her tight bodice. "They want *out* of this gown."

"For pity's sake, Eugenia!" The duchess shot a glance at the stony-faced limo driver. "Let's continue this discussion tomorrow, shall we?"

Nodding, Gina bent to kiss her grandmother's cheek and breathed in the faint, oh-so-familiar scent of lavender and lace. "Make sure you take your medicine before you go to bed."

"I'm not senile, young lady. I think I can manage to remember to take two little pills."

"Yes, ma'am."

Trying to look properly chastised, she helped the duchess into the limo and turned to the Honduran native who'd become a second mother to her and Sarah. "You'll stay with her, Maria? I shouldn't be more than another hour or two. I'll have a car take you home."

"Take as long as you need. *La duquesa* and I, we'll put our feet up and talk about what a fine job you did organizing such a beautiful wedding."

"It did come off well, didn't it?"

Maria beamed a wide smile. "*Sí, chica,* it did."

Buoyed by the compliment, Gina returned to the reception room. Most of the guests had departed. Including, she saw after a quick sweep, a certain obnoxious ambassador who'd shown up unexpectedly. She should have had him escorted out when he first walked in. Being summarily ejected from the wedding would have put a dent in the man's ego. Or maybe not. For a career diplomat, he seemed as impervious to Gina's snubs as to her adamant refusal to marry him.

He didn't understand why she wouldn't even consider it for their baby's sake. Neither did the duchess. Although Grandmama and Sarah both supported Gina's decision to go it alone, she knew they wondered at her vehemence. On the surface, John Harris Mason III certainly made excellent husband material. He was rich, handsome and charming as the devil when he wanted to be.

It was what lurked below the surface that held Gina back. Every story, every bio printed about the charismatic diplomat, hinted that Jack had buried his heart with the young wife he'd first dated in high school and married the day they both graduated from Harvard. From all reports, Catherine Mason had been every bit as smart, athletic and politically involved as her husband.

Gina knew in her heart she couldn't compete with the ghost of his lost love. Not because she lacked her own set of credentials. The Duchy of Karlenburgh might now be little more than an obscure footnote in history books, but Grandmama could still hold her own with presidents and kings. What's more, she'd insisted her granddaughters be educated in accordance with their heritage. Gina had actually graduated from Barnard with a semi-decent grade point average.

She'd pretty much majored in partying, though, and to this day had zero interest in politics.

She might have cultivated an interest for Jack. Had actually toyed with the idea during that crazy weekend. For all her seemingly casual approach to life and love, she'd never met anyone as fascinating and entertaining and just plain hot as Jack Mason.

Any thoughts of fitting into the mold of a diplomat's wife went poof when Gina discovered she was pregnant. There was no way she could dive into politics *and* marriage *and* motherhood at the same time. She already felt as though she were on an emotional roller coaster. All she could think about right now, all she would *allow* herself to think about, was proving she could take care of herself and her baby.

"You put on a helluva party, lady."

Smiling, she turned to Dev's gravel-voiced buddy from his air force days. Patrick Donovan now served as Dev's executive assistant and pretty much ruled his vast empire with an iron fist.

"Thanks, Pat."

Tall and lanky and looking completely at home in his Armani tux, Donovan winked at her. "You decide you want to come back to L.A., you let me know. We could use someone with your organizational skills in our protocol office. Seems like we're hosting some bigwig industrialists from China or Germany or Australia every other week."

"I appreciate the offer but I'm going to try to break into the event-planning business here in New York. Plus, I'm thinking about moving in with Grandmama for the next eight months or so."

If the duchess would have her. They'd all been so busy these past few weeks with Sarah's wedding, Gina hadn't found the right time to broach the subject. Her sister heartily endorsed the plan, though. Both she and Gina hated the thought of the duchess living alone now that Sarah was moving out.

Okay! All right! So Gina needed a place to stay until she landed a job and became self-supporting. Despite her determination to prove herself, she had to have a base to build on. Grandmama wouldn't object to letting her move in. Probably.

"I've got some pretty good contacts in New York," Patrick was saying. "You want me to make a few calls? Grease the skids a little?"

"I need to do this on my own, Pat. But thanks for the offer."

"It stays on the table," he said with a shrug as he wrapped an arm around her shoulders and gave her a squeeze. "Call me if you change your mind. Or better yet, let your new brother-in-law know. Dev is complete mush right now. He'd set you up with your own agency if you so much as hint that's what you want. And let me know if you want me to close up your apartment in L.A. and have your things shipped here."

"I will. Thanks again."

Gina climbed out of a cab some two hours later. The Dakota's red sandstone turrets poked against the darkening night sky, welcoming her to the castlelike apartment complex that was one of New York City's most prestigious addresses. The duchess had bought an apartment here shortly after arriving in New York City. The purchase had put a serious dent in her cache of jewels, but careful investments during those first years, along with the discreet sale of a diamond bracelet here, a ruby necklace there, had allowed Charlotte to maintain the apartment and an elegant lifestyle over the decades.

Keeping up the facade had become much tougher in recent years. The jewels were gone. So were most of the haute couture gowns and designer suits that once filled her grandmother's closet. With her love of the classic retro look, Sarah had salvaged a number of the outfits and saved money by not splurging on new clothes for herself, but she'd had to struggle to cover the bills from her own salary.

Dev, bless him, wanted to make things easier for his wife's grandmother. But like the wedding expenses, taking over the duchess's financial affairs involved delicate negotiations that had yet to reach a satisfactory conclusion. Which put the burden on Gina's shoulders. She couldn't just move in and expect her grandmother to support her. She had to pay her own way.

On that determined note, she thanked Maria for staying so late and told her to sleep in the next morning. "I'll make breakfast for Grandmama."

The Honduran looked dubious. "Are you sure, *chica? La duquesa,* she likes her egg poached just so."

"I know. It has to sit for exactly four minutes after the heat's turned off."

"And her tea. It must be…"

"The Twinings English Black. I've got it covered. The car's waiting for you. Go home and get some rest."

Maria obviously had her doubts but gathered her suitcase-sized purse. "I'll see you tomorrow."

Gina was up and waiting when her grandmother walked into the kitchen just after eight-thirty the next morning. The duchess was impeccably dressed as always in a calf-length black skirt and lavender silk overblouse. Her hair formed its usual, neat snowy crown atop her head, but Gina saw with a quick dart of concern that she was leaning more heavily than she normally did on her cane.

"Good morning," she said, masking her worry behind a cheerful smile. "I got a text from Sarah a while ago. She says it's balmy and beautiful in Majorca."

"I expect it is. Are you doing breakfast?"

"I am. Sit, and I'll bring your tea."

Surprised and just a little wary, the duchess seated herself in the sunny breakfast room off the kitchen. Its ivy-sprigged wallpaper, green seat cushions and windows overlooking

Central Park seemed to bring the bright May spring right into the room.

Gina poured hot water over the leaves she'd measured into her grandmother's favorite Wedgwood teapot and placed the pot on the table. While the Twinings Black steeped, she popped some wheat bread in the toaster and brought a saucepan of water back to a boil before easing two raw eggs out of their shells. The sight of the yolks gave her a moment's qualm, but it passed. Still no twinge of morning nausea, thank God! With any luck, she'd escape that scourge altogether.

"Here we are."

She hadn't kept the yolks from breaking and going all runny, but the duchess thanked her with a smile and buttered her toast. Sensing there was something behind this special effort, she munched delicately on a corner of toast and waited patiently.

Gina pulled in a deep breath and took the plunge. "I was wondering, Grandmama…"

Dang! Admitting she was a screwup and needed to come live with her grandmother until she got her life in order was harder than she'd anticipated.

"I thought perhaps I might stay with you until I get a job. If you don't mind, that is."

"Oh, Eugenia!" Charlotte's reaction came swift and straight from the heart. "Of course I don't mind, my darling girl. This is your home. You must stay for as long as you wish. You and the baby."

Gina wasn't crying. She really wasn't. The tears just sort of leaked through her smile. "Thanks, Grandmama."

Her own lips a little wobbly, the duchess reached for her granddaughter's hand. "I admit I wasn't looking forward to rattling around this place by myself now that Sarah's moving out. I'm delighted you want to stay here. Will you need to fly back to L.A. to pack up your things?"

"Dev's assistant, Patrick, said he would take care of that if I decided to stay in New York."

"Good!" Charlotte gave her hand a quick squeeze and picked up her fork. "Now, what's this Sarah told me about you wanting to go into the catering business?"

"Not catering. Event planning. I did a little of it in L.A. Just enough to know I'm better at organizing and throwing parties than…" She managed a watery chuckle. "Than everything else I've tried."

"Well, you certainly did an excellent job with the wedding."

The praise sent Gina's spirits winging. "I did, didn't I?" She preened for a moment, her tears forgotten. "And the photographer from Sarah's magazine shot some amazing video and stills. He gave me a disk with enough material to put together a portfolio. I just emailed it to the woman I'm interviewing with this afternoon."

Her grandmother paused with her fork halfway to her lips. "You have an interview this afternoon?"

"I do. With Nicole Tremayne, head of the Tremayne Group. TTG operates a dozen different event venues, three right here in the city."

"Hmm. I knew a Nicholas Tremayne some years ago. Quite well, actually." Her thoughts seemed to go inward for a moment. Shaking them off, she lowered her fork. "This Nicole must be his daughter. If so, I'll call him and…"

"No, Grandmama, please don't."

The urgent plea brought a look of surprise. "Why ever not?"

"I want to do this on my own."

"That sentiment does you justice, Eugenia, but…"

"You don't have to say it. I know my track record doesn't suggest I'll make a very reliable employee. When you add the fact that I'm pregnant, it'll be a miracle if I land any job. I want to try, though, Grandmama. I really do."

"Very well. I'll refrain from interfering."

"Thank you. Dev and Patrick made the same promise. And I'll get Jack to do the same when I meet him for lunch today."

The duchess tilted her head. Sudden interest gleamed in her faded blue eyes. "You're having lunch with Jack? Why? I thought you'd said all you have to say to him."

"I did. Several times! The man won't take no for an answer."

"So again I ask, why are you having lunch with him?"

"He badgered me into it," Gina admitted in disgust. "You can see why I don't want to marry him."

The duchess took her time replying. When she did, she chose her words carefully.

"Are you sure, Eugenia? I treasure every moment I had with your mother and with you and Sarah, but I speak from experience when I say raising a child on your own can be quite terrifying at times."

"Oh, Grandmama!"

Her eyes misted again. Blinking furiously, Gina bared her soul. "I'm scared out my gourd. I admit it! The only thing that makes me even think I can do this is you, and the love you lavished on Sarah and me. You filled our lives with such joy, such grand adventures. You still do. I can give that to my child. I know I can."

A smile started in her grandmother's eyes and spread to Gina's heart.

"I know you can, too."

Gina had intended to spend the rest of the morning prepping for her interview with Nicole Tremayne. To her annoyance, her thoughts kept slipping away from party planning and instead landed on Jack Mason.

Her irritation increased even more when she found herself scowling at the few outfits she'd brought to New York with her. They were all flashy, all playful. Thigh-skimming skirts in bold prints. Tights in eye-popping colors. Spangled, midriff-baring T-shirts. Reflective of her personality, maybe, but not the image she wanted to project to Ms. Tremayne. Or to a certain ambassador-at-large.

Abandoning the meager offering, she went next door to Sarah's room and rummaged through the designer classics her sister had salvaged from their grandmother's closet. After much debate and a pile of discards strewn across the bed, Gina decided on wide-legged black slacks. She topped them with a summer silk Valentino jacket in pearl gray that boasted a flower in the same fabric on one lapel. The jacket strained a bit at the bust but gave her the mature, responsible air she was aiming for. A wad of cotton stuffed into the toes of a pair of sensible black pumps added to the look. As a final touch, she went light on the makeup and wrestled her waterfall of platinum-blond curls into a French twist. When she studied the final result in the mirror, she gulped.

"Oh, God. I look like Grandmama."

If the duchess recognized herself, she mercifully refrained from saying so. But Gina caught the slightly stunned look she exchanged with Maria as her new, subdued granddaughter departed for her lunch meeting.

If Gina had needed further evidence of her transformation, she got it mere moments after walking into the Boathouse. A favorite gathering place of tourists and locals alike, the restaurant's floor-to-ceiling windows gave unimpeded views of the rowboats and gondolas gliding across Central Park's Reservoir Lake. Both the lake and the trees surrounding it were showcased against the dramatic backdrop of the Manhattan skyline.

The Boathouse's casual bar and restaurant buzzed with a crowd dressed in everything from business to smart casual to just plain comfortable. Despite the logjam, Gina spotted Jack immediately. As promised, he'd secured a table tucked in a quiet corner that still gave an unobstructed view of the lake. She stood for a moment at the top of the short flight of steps leading down to the dining area and put a hand on the railing to steady herself.

Oh, Lord! Her hormones must be cartwheeling again. Why else would her knees get all wobbly at the way the sunlight streaked his tawny hair? Or her lungs wheeze like an old accordion at the sight of his strong, tanned hands holding up a menu? In the tux he'd worn to the wedding yesterday, Jack had wreaked havoc on her emotions. In a crisply starched pale blue shirt with the cuffs rolled up on muscled forearms lightly sprinkled with gold fuzz, he almost opened the floodgates.

She was still clinging to the wooden rail when he glanced up. His gaze swept the entrance area from left to right. Passed over her. Jerked back. He was too polished a diplomat to reveal more than a flash of surprise, but that brief glimpse gave Gina the shot in the arm she needed. Channeling the duchess at her most regal, she smiled at the head waiter, who hurried over to assist her.

"May I show you to a table?"

"Thank you, but I see the party I'm meeting."

She tipped her chin toward Jack, now rising from his chair. The waiter followed her gaze and offered a hand.

"Yes, of course. Please, watch your step."

Jack had recovered from his momentary surprise. Gina wasn't sure she liked the amusement that replaced it.

"I almost didn't recognize you," he admitted. "Are you going for a new look?"

"As a matter of fact, I am."

She took the seat next to him and considered how much to share of her plans. After a swift internal debate, she decided it might be good to let him know that she did, in fact, have plans.

"I'm also going for a new career. I have a job interview this afternoon with the head of the Tremayne Group. TTG is one of the biggest event-coordinating companies in the business, with venues in New York, Washington and Chicago."

The change in Jack was so subtle she almost missed it. Just a slight stiffening of his shoulders. She bristled, thinking he was going to object to her making a foray into the professional party world while carrying his child. Instead, he responded quietly, calmly.

"TTG also has a venue in Boston. My wife used them to coordinate our wedding."

Three

"Oh, Jack!"

Gina's soft heart turned instantly to mush. She didn't want to marry this man but neither did she want to hurt him. Ignoring the obvious inconsistency in that thought, she dug in her purse for her cell phone.

"I'm sorry. I didn't know you had that connection to TTG. I'll call and cancel my interview."

"Wait." Frowning, he put a hand on her arm. "I'll admit I would prefer not to see you pursue a career here in New York. Or anywhere else, for that matter. But…"

"But?"

Still frowning, he searched her face. "Are you really dead set against marriage, Gina?"

Her gaze dropped to his hand, so strong and tan against the paler skin of her forearm. The stress and confusion of the past weeks made a jumble of her reply.

"Sort of."

"What does that mean?"

She looked up and met his serious brown eyes. "I like you, Jack. When you're not coming on all huffy and autocratic, that is. And God knows we were fantastic together in bed."

So fantastic she had to slam the door on the images that thought conjured up.

"But I think...I know we both want more in a marriage."

He was silent, and Gina gathered her courage.

"Tell me about your wife. What was she like?"

He sat back, withdrawing his hand in the process. Withdrawing himself, as well. His glance shifted to the rowboats circling the lake. The ripples from their oars distorted the reflected images of the high-rises peeking above Central Park's leafy green tree line. The buildings seemed to sway on the lake's blue-green surface.

"Catherine was funny and smart and had a killer serve," he said finally, turning back to Gina. "She cleaned my clock every time we got on a tennis court. She might have turned pro if she hadn't lived, breathed and slept politics."

The waiter appeared at that moment. Gina ordered decaffeinated mango tea, Jack a refill of his coffee. They listened to the specials and let the menus sit on the table after the waiter withdrew. She was afraid the interruption had broken the thread of a conversation she knew had to be painful, but Jack picked it up again.

"Catherine and another campaign worker were going door-to-door to canvas unregistered voters for the presidential campaign. She suffered a brain aneurysm and collapsed. The docs say she was dead before she hit the sidewalk."

"I'm so sorry."

"We didn't learn until after the autopsy that she had Ehlers-Danlos syndrome. It's a rare, inherited condition that can cause the walls of your blood vessels to rupture. Which," he said as he eased a leather portfolio out from under his menu, "is why I prepared this."

"This" turned out to be a set of stapled papers. For a wild moment Gina thought they might be a prenup. Or a copy of a will, naming the baby as his heir if he should die as unexpectedly as Catherine had. Or...

"Your obstetrician will want a complete medical history

of both parents," he said calmly. "As far as I know, I haven't inherited any rare diseases but my father and grandfather both suffer from chronic high blood pressure and my mother is a breast cancer survivor. Who's your doctor, by the way?"

"I don't have one yet."

The frown came back. "Why the delay? You should've had your first prenatal checkup by now."

"It's on my list, right after getting resettled in New York and finding a job."

"Move the obstetrician to the top of the list," he ordered, switching into his usual take-charge mode. "I'll cover your medical expenses until you land a job."

"No, Mr. Ambassador, you won't."

"Oh, for…!"

He dropped the papers, closed his eyes for a moment and adopted a calm, soothing tone that made Gina want to hiss.

"Let's just talk this through. You're currently unemployed. I assume you have no health insurance. Few obstetricians will take you on as a patient unless there's some guarantee you can pay for their services."

"I. Will. Find. A. Job."

"Okay, okay." He held up a placating hand. "Even if you do land a job in the next few days or weeks, health benefits probably won't kick in for at least six months. And then they may not cover preexisting conditions."

Well, crap! Gina hadn't considered that. Her throat closed as her carefully constructed house of cards seemed to teeter and topple right before her eyes.

No! No, dammit! Hormones or no hormones, she would not break down and bawl in front of Jack.

He must have sensed her fierce struggle for control. His expression softened, and he dropped the grating, let's-be-reasonable tone. "This is my baby, too, Gina. Let me help however I can."

She could handle autocratic and obnoxious. Nice was

harder to manager. Shoving back her chair, she pushed away from the table.

"I have to go to the bathroom."

After some serious soul-searching, she returned from the ladies' room to find the waiter had delivered their drinks. Gina dumped artificial sweetener in her tea and took a fortifying sip before acknowledging the unpalatable truth.

"I guess I didn't think this whole insurance thing through. If it turns out I can't get medical benefits in time to cover my appointments with an obstetrician, I would appreciate your help."

"You've got it." He hesitated a moment before extending another offer. "Finding a good doctor isn't easy, especially with everything else you have going on right now. Why don't I call my chief of staff and have him email you a list of the top OB docs in the city? He can also verify that they're accepting new patients."

And coordinate the payment process, Gina guessed. Swallowing her pride, she nodded. "I'd appreciate that."

"Just call me when you decide on a doctor. Or call Dale Vickers, my chief of staff. He'll make sure your appointments get on my schedule."

"Your schedule?"

"I'll fly up from D.C. to go with you, of course. Assuming I'm in the country."

"Oh. Of course."

The sense that she could do this on her own was rapidly slipping away. Trying desperately to hang on to her composure, Gina picked up her menu.

"We'd better order. My appointment at the Tremayne Group is at two-thirty."

Jack's hand hovered over his menu. "This might sound a little crass but between Catherine's family and mine, we spent an obscene amount of money on our wedding. I could make a call and…"

"No!"

Gina gritted her teeth. Was she the only person in the whole friggin' universe who didn't have an inside connection at TTG? And the only fool who refused to exploit that connection? Sheer stubbornness had her shaking her head.

"No calls. No pulling strings. No playing the big ambassadorial cheese. I have to do this myself."

He lifted a tawny brow but didn't press the point. After signaling the waiter over to take their orders, he steered the conversation into more neutral channels.

The awkwardness of the situation eased, and Gina's spirits took an upward swing. Jack soon had her laughing at some of his more humorous exploits in the field and realizing once again how charming he could be when he wanted to.

And sexy. So damned sexy. She savored the lump crab cake she'd ordered for lunch and couldn't help admiring the way the tanned skin at the corners of his eyes crinkled when he smiled. And how the light reflecting off the lake added glints to the sun-streaked gold of his hair. When he leaned forward, Gina caught the ripple of muscle under his starched shirt. She found herself remembering how she'd run her palms over all that hard muscle. That tight butt. Those iron thighs. The bunched biceps and…

"Gina?"

She almost choked on a lump of crab. "Sorry. What were you saying?"

"I was asking if you'd consider coming down to D.C. for a short visit. I'd like to show you my home and introduce you to my parents."

The request was reasonable. Naturally Jack's parents would want to meet the mother of their grandchild. From the little he'd let drop about his staunchly conservative father, though, Gina suspected John Harris Mason II probably wouldn't greet her with open arms.

"Let's talk about that later," she hedged. "After I get settled and find a job."

They finished lunch and lingered a few minutes over tea and coffee refills. Gina's nerves had started to get jittery by the time they exited the Boathouse. Jack walked with her through the park now filled with bicyclers and in-line skaters and sun worshippers sprawled on benches with eyes closed and faces tilted to the sky.

A group of Japanese tourists had congregated at Bethesda Fountain and were busy snapping photos of each other with the bronze statue of the *Angel of the Waters* towering over them. At the shy request of one of the younger members of the group, Jack obligingly stopped to take a picture of the whole party. Everyone wanted a copy on their own camera so Gina ended up acting as a runner, passing him ten or twelve cameras before they were done. By the time they reached Fifth Avenue and Jack hailed a cab to take her to her interview, she was feeling the pressure of time.

"Keep your fingers crossed," she said without thinking as the cab pulled over to the curb.

Only as he reached to open the door for her did she remember that he would prefer she didn't land this—or any job—in New York. He made no secret of the fact that he wanted to put a ring on her finger and take care of her and their child. To his credit, he buried those feelings behind an easy smile.

"I'll do better than that. Here's a kiss for luck."

He kept it light. Just a brush of his lips over hers. On the first pass, at least.

Afterward Gina could never say for sure who initiated the second pass. All she knew was that Jack hooked a hand behind her nape, she went up on tiptoe and what had started as a friendly good-luck token got real deep and real hungry.

When he finally raised his head, she saw herself reflected in his eyes. "I…I have to go!"

He stepped back and gave her room to make an escape. She slid into the cab and spent the short drive to the Tremayne Group's headquarters trying desperately to remember all the reasons why she wanted—no, needed!—this job.

* * *

At three-ten, she was reiterating that same grim list. She'd been sitting in Nicole Tremayne's ultramodern outer office for more than half an hour while a harried receptionist fielded phone calls and a succession of subordinates rushed in and out of the boss's office. Any other time Gina would have walked out after the first fifteen or twenty minutes. She didn't have that luxury now.

Instead, she'd used the time to reread the information she'd found on Google about the Tremayne Group. She also studied every page in the slick, glossy brochure given out to prospective clients. Even then she had to unlock her jaw and force a smile when the receptionist finally ushered her into the inner sanctum.

Stunned, Gina stopped dead. This dark cavern was the command center of a company that hosted more than two thousand events a year at a dozen different venues? And this tiny whirlwind erupting from behind her marble slab of a desk was the famed Nicole Tremayne?

She couldn't have been more than five-one, and she owed at least four of those inches to her needle-heeled ankle boots. Gina was still trying to marry the bloodred ankle boots to her salt-and-pepper corkscrew curls when Nicole thrust out a hand.

"Sorry to keep you waiting. You're Eugenia, right? Eugenia St. Sebastian?"

"Yes, I…"

"My father had a thing for your grandmother. I was just a kid at the time, but I remember he talked about leaving my mother for her."

"Oh. Well, uh…"

"He should have. My mother was a world-class ball-breaker." Swooping a thick book of fabric swatches off one of the chairs in front of her desk, Tremayne dumped it on the floor. "Sit, sit."

Still slightly stunned, Gina sat. Nicole cleared the chair

next to hers and perched on its edge with the nervous energy of a hummingbird.

"I looked at the digital portfolio of your sister's wedding. Classy job. You did all the arrangements?"

"With some help."

"Who from?"

"Andrew, at the Plaza. And Patrick Donovan. He's..."

"Dev Hunter's right-hand man. I know. We coordinated a major charity event for Hunter's corporation last year. Three thousand attendees at two thousand a pop. So when can you start?"

"Excuse me?"

"One of the assistant event planners at our midtown venue just got busted for possession. She's out on bail, but I can't have a user working for TTG." Her bird-bright eyes narrowed on Gina. "You don't do dope, do you?"

"No."

"I'd better not find out otherwise."

"You won't."

Tremayne nodded. "Here's the thing. You have a lousy work record but a terrific pedigree. If you inherited half your grandmother's class and a quarter of her smarts, you should be able to handle this job."

Gina wasn't sure whether she'd just been complimented or insulted. She was still trying to decide when her prospective boss continued briskly.

"You also grew up here in the city. You know your way around and you know how to interact with the kind of customers we attract. Plus, the classy digital portfolio you sent me shows you've got a flair for design and know computers. Whether you can handle vendors and show yourself as a team player remains to be seen, but I'm willing to give you a shot. When can you start?"

Tomorrow!

The joyous reply was almost out before Gina caught it. Gulping, she throttled back her exhilaration.

"I can start anytime but there's something I need to tell you before we go any further."

"What's that?"

"I'm pregnant."

"And I'm Episcopalian. So?"

Could it really be this easy? Gina didn't think so. Suspicion wormed through her elation.

"Did my grandmother call you?" she asked. "Or Pat Donovan?"

"No."

Her jaw locked. Dammit! It had to have been Jack.

"Then I assume you talked to the ambassador," she said stiffly.

"What ambassador?"

"Jack Mason."

"Jack Mason." Tremayne tapped her chin with a nail shellacked the same red as her ankle boots. "Why do I know that name?"

Gina didn't mention that TTG had coordinated Jack's wedding. For reasons she would have to sort out later, that cut too close to the bone.

"Who is he," Tremayne asked, "and why would he call me?"

"He's a friend." That was the best she could come up with. "I told him about our interview and…and thought he might have called to weigh in."

"Well, it certainly never hurts to have an ambassador in your corner, but no, he didn't call me. So what's the deal here? Do you want the job or not?"

There were probably a dozen different questions she should ask before jumping into the fray. Like how much the job paid, for one. And what her hours would be. And whether the position came with benefits. At the moment, though, Gina was too jazzed to voice any of the questions buzzing around in her head.

"Yes, ma'am, I do."

"Good. Have my assistant direct you to the woman who handles our personnel matters. You can fill out all the necessary forms there. And call me Nikki," she added as her new employee sprang out of her chair to shake on the deal.

Gina left the Tremayne Group's personnel office thirty or forty forms later. The salary was less than she'd hoped for but the description of her duties made her grin. As assistant events coordinator she would be involved in all phases of operation for TTG's midtown venue. Scheduling parties and banquets and trade shows. Devising themes to fit the clients' desires. Creating menus. Contracting with vendors to supply food and decorations and bar stock. Arranging for limos, for security, for parking.

Even better, the personnel officer had stressed that there was plenty of room for advancement within TTG. The tantalizing prospect of a promotion danced before Gina's eyes as she exited the high-rise housing the company's headquarters. When she hit the still glorious May sunshine, she had to tell someone her news. Her first, almost instinctive, impulse was to call Jack. She actually had her iPhone in hand before she stopped to wonder why.

Simple answer. She wanted to crow a little.

Not so simple answer. She wanted to prove she wasn't all fun and fluff.

With a wry grimace, she acknowledged that she should probably wait until she'd actually performed in her new position for a few weeks or months before she made that claim. She decided to text Sarah instead. The message was short and sweet.

I'm now a working mom-to-be. Call when you and Dev come up for air.

She took a cab back to the Upper West Side and popped out at a deli a few blocks from the Dakota. Osterman's had occupied the same choice corner location since the Great Depression. Gina and Sarah had developed their passion for corned beef at the deli's tiny, six-table eating area. The sisters still indulged whenever they were in the city, but Gina's target tonight was the case displaying Osterman's world famous cheesecakes. With unerring accuracy, she went for a selection that included her own, her grandmother's and Maria's favorites.

"One slice each of the white chocolate raspberry truffle, the key lime and the Dutch apple caramel, please. And one pineapple upside down," she added on an afterthought.

The boxed cheesecake wedges in hand, she plucked a bottle of chilled champagne from the cooler in the wine corner. She had to search for a nonalcoholic counterpart but finally found it in with the fruit juices. Driven by the urge to celebrate, she added a wedge of aged brie and a loaf of crusty bread to her basket. On her way to check out she passed a shelf containing the deli's selection of caviars.

The sticker price of a four-ounce jar of Caspian Sea Osetra made her gasp. Drawing in a steadying breath, she reminded herself it was Grandmama's caviar of choice. The duchess considered Beluga too salty and Sevruga too fishy. Gina made a quick calculation and decided her credit card would cover the cost of one jar. Maybe.

"Oh, what the hell."

To her relief, she got out of Osterman's without having the credit card confiscated. A block and a half later she approached the Dakota with all her purchases.

"Let me help you with those!"

The doorman who'd held his post for as long as she could remember leaped forward. Although she would never say so to his face, Gina suspected Jerome assumed his present duties about the same time Osterman's opened its doors.

"You should have called a cab, Lady Eugenia."

Sarah and Gina had spent most of their adult years trying to get Jerome to drop their empty titles. They'd finally agreed it was a wasted effort.

"I'm okay," Gina protested as he tried to relieve her of her burdens. "Except for this."

She sorted through her purchases and fished out a wedge-shaped box. Jerome peeked inside and broke into a grin.

"Pineapple upside down! Trust you to remember my favorite."

Gina's emotions jumped on the roller coaster again as she thought about his devoted loyalty to her and Grandmama over the years.

"How could I forget?" she said with a suspicious catch to her voice. "You slipped me an extra few dollars every time I said I was going to Osterman's."

For a moment she thought the embarrassed doorman would pat her on the head as he'd done so many times when she was a child. He controlled the impulse and commented instead on the bottles poking out of her bag.

"Still celebrating Lady Sarah's wedding?"

"Nope. This celebration is in my honor."

Riding her emotional roller coaster to its gravity-defying apex, she poured out her news.

"I'm moving back to New York, Jerome."

"Lady Eugenia! That's wonderful news. I admit I was a bit worried about the duchess."

"There's more. I've got a job."

"Good for you."

"Oh," she added over her shoulder as she made for the lobby. "I'm also pregnant."

Four

Gina walked into the Tremayne Group's midtown venue at 9:30 a.m. the next morning. She didn't drag out again until well past midnight.

Her first impression was *wow!* What had once been a crumbling brick warehouse overlooking the East River was now a glass-fronted, ultra-high-rent complex of offices, restaurants and entertainment venues. TTG occupied a slightly recessed four-story suite smack in the center of the complex. The primo location allowed into a private ground-floor courtyard with bubbling fountains and a top-floor terrace that had to offer magnificent views of the river.

A young woman with wings of blue in her otherwise lipstick-red hair sat at a curved glass reception desk and fielded phone calls. Gina waited until she finished with one caller and put two others on hold to introduce herself.

"I'm Gina St. Sebastian. I'm the new..."

"Assistant coordinator. Thank God you're here! I'm Kallie. Samuel's in the banquet hall. He said to send you right up. Third floor. The elevators are to your right."

Gina used the ride to do a quick check in mirrored panels. She'd left her hair down today but confined the silky curls behind a wide fuchsia headband studded with crystals. A belt in the same hot pink circled the waist of her apple-green J. Crew tunic. Since this was her first day on the job she'd gone with sedate black tights instead of the colorful prints she preferred. She made a quick swipe with her lip gloss and drew in a deep, steadying breath. Then the elevator door glided open and she stepped out into a vortex of sound and fury.

What looked like a small army of workers in blue overalls was yanking folded chairs from metal-sided carrier racks, popping them open and thumping them around a room full of circluar tables. Another crew, this one in black pants and white shirts, scurried after the first. They draped each chair in shimmering green, the tables in cloth of gold. Right behind them came yet another crew rattling down place settings of china and crystal. The *rat-tat-tat* of staple guns fired by intent set designers erecting a fantastic Emerald City added to the barrage of noise, while the heady scent of magnolias wafted from dozens of tall topiaries stacked on carts waiting to be rolled to the tables.

Soaking up the energy like a sponge, Gina wove her way through the tables to a wild-haired broomstick with a clipboard in one hand, a walkie-talkie in the other and a Bluetooth headset hooked over one ear. "Not *The Wizard of Oz,*" he was shouting into the headset. "Christ, who does Judy Garland anymore? This is the new movie. *Oz the... Oz the...*"

Scowling, he snapped his fingers at Gina.

"Oz the Great and Powerful," she dutifully asserted.

"Right. *Oz the Great and Powerful.* It's a Disney flick starring Rachel Weisz and..."

More finger snaps.

"Mila Kunis."

"Right. Mila Kunis. That's the music the clients requested." The scowl deepened. "Hell, no, I don't! Hold on."

He whipped his head around and barked at Gina. "You the new AC?"

"Yes."

"I'm Samuel DeGrange."

"Nice to…"

He brushed aside the pleasantries with an impatient hand. "Go upstairs and tell the DJ to pull his head out of his ass. The clients don't want Dorothy and Toto, for God's sake! Then make sure the bar supervisor knows how to mix the fizzy green juice concoction that's supposed to make the kids think they're dancing down a new, improved Yellow Brick Road."

Eight and a half hours later Gina was zipped into the Glinda the Good Witch costume that had been rented for her predecessor and making frantic last-minute changes to seating charts. Kallie the receptionist—now garbed as a munchkin—wielded a calligraphy pen to scribble out place cards for the twenty additional guests the honoree's mother had somehow forgotten she'd invited until she was in the limo and on her way from Temple with the newly bat mitzvahed Rachel.

Another six hours later, Gina collapsed into a green-draped chair and gazed at the rubble. Iridescent streamers in green and gold littered the dance floor. Scattered among them was a forgotten emerald tiara here, an empty party-favors box there. The booths where the seventy-five kids invited to celebrate Rachel's coming of age had fired green lasers and demolished video villains were being dismantled. Only a few crumbs remained of the fourteen-layer cake with its glittering towers and turrets. The kids invited to the party had devoured it with almost as much gusto as the more than two hundred parents, grandparents, aunts, uncles, cousins and family friends had drained the open bar upstairs.

Gina stretched out her feet in their glittery silver slippers and aimed a grin at the toothpick-thin Tin Man who flopped into the chair beside her.

"This party business is fun."

"You think?" Samuel shoved back his tin hat and gave her a jaundiced smile. "Talk to me again after you've had an inebriated best man puke all over you. Or spent two hours sifting through piles of garbage to find a guest's diamond-and-sapphire earrings. Which, incidentally, she calls to tell you she found in her purse."

"At least she let you know she found it," Gina replied, laughing.

"She's one of the few. Seems like our insurance rates take another jump after every event." He slanted her a sideways glance. "You did good tonight, St. Sebastian. Better than I expected when I read your resumé."

"Thanks. I think."

"You need to keep a closer finger on the pulse of the party, though. The natives got a little restless before the cake was brought out."

Gina bit her lip. No need to remind her new boss that he'd sent her out to the terrace to shepherd some underage smokers back inside right when the cake was supposed to have been presented.

"I'll watch the timing," she promised.

"So go home now. I'll do the final bar count and leave this mess to the cleaning crew."

She wasn't about to argue. "I'll see you tomorrow."

"Nine sharp," he warned. "We've got a preliminary wedding consult. I'll talk, you listen and learn."

She popped a salute. "Yes, sir."

"Christ! You got enough energy left for that?" He didn't wait for an answer, just shooed her away. "Get out of here."

The *Oz the Great and Powerful* bat mitzvah set the stage for the dozens of events that followed during the busy, busy month of May. Almost before she knew it Gina was caught up in a whirl of wedding and engagement and anniversary and graduation and coming-of-age parties. She gained both experience and confidence with each event.

So much so that Samuel soon delegated full responsibility for computing and placing orders with the subs for everything from decorations to bar stock. He also tapped her for fresh ideas for themes and settings. In rapid succession she helped plan a white-on-white wedding, a red-and-black "Puttin' on the Ritz" debutante ball and a barefoot-on-the-beach engagement party at a private Hamptons estate. And then there was her grand coup—snaring Justin Bieber for a brief appearance at the national Girl Scout banquet to be held in the fall. He was in town for another event and Gina played shamelessly on his agent's heartstrings until every teen's favorite heartthrob agreed.

Not all events went smoothly. Frantically working her cell phone and walkie-talkie, Gina learned to cope with minor crises like a forgotten kosher meal for the rabbi, a groom caught frolicking in the fourth-floor bridal suite shower with the maid of honor and a drunken guest held hostage by an irate limo driver demanding payment for damage done to the vehicle's leather seats.

In the midst of all the craziness she unpacked the boxes Dev's assistant had shipped back from L.A. and welcomed her sister and her new brother-in-law home from their honeymoon. Gina and Sarah and the duchess were all teary-eyed when the newlyweds departed again, this time to look at homes for sale close to Dev's corporate headquarters in California.

Miracle of miracles, Gina also managed to snag an appointment with the top OB doc on the short list of three Jack had emailed. She suspected he'd used his influence or family clout to make sure she got in to see one of them. She didn't object to outside help in this instance. The health of her baby took precedence over pride.

As promised, she called Jack's office to let him know about the appointment. A secretary routed her to his chief of staff.

"This is Dale Vickers, Ms. St. Sebastian. The ambassador is in conference. May I help you?"

"Jack asked me to let him know the date and time of my prenatal appointment. It's Thursday of next week, at three-fifteen, with Dr. Sondra Martinson."

"I'm looking at his calendar now. The ambassador is unavailable next Thursday. Please reschedule the appointment and call me back."

The reply was as curt as it was officious. Gina held out the phone and looked at it in surprise for a moment before putting it to her ear again.

"Tell you what," she said, oozing sweetness and light, "just tell Jack to call me. We'll take it from there."

The man must have realized his mistake. Softening his tone, he tried to regain lost ground.

"I'm sorry if I sounded abrupt, Ms. St. Sebastian. It's just that the ambassador is participating all next week in a conference with senior State Department officials. They're assessing U.S. embassy security in light of recent terrorist attacks. I can't overstate the importance of this conference to the safety and security of our consular personnel abroad."

Properly put in her place, Gina was about to concede the point when he made a suggestion.

"Why don't I call Dr. Martinson's office and arrange an appointment that fits with the ambassador's schedule?"

"That won't work. We need to work around my schedule, too."

"I'm sure you can squeeze something in between parties for twelve-year-olds."

The barely disguised put-down dropped Gina's jaw. What was with this character? Sheer obstinacy had her oozing even more saccharine.

"I'm sure I can. After all, the tab for our last twelve-year-old's party only ran to sixty-five thousand dollars and change. Just have Jack call me. We'll work something out."

"Really, Ms. St. Sebastian, we don't have to trouble the ambassador with such a trivial matter."

Heat shot to every one of Gina's extremities. Given her normally sunny and fun-loving disposition, she'd never believed that old cliché about seeing red. She did now.

"Listen, asshole, you may consider the ambassador's baby a trivial matter. I'm pretty sure he won't agree. The appointment is for three-fifteen next Thursday. End of discussion."

As instructed, she arrived at Dr. Martinson's office a half hour prior to her scheduled appointment. The time was required for a final review and signature on the forms she'd downloaded from the office website. She hadn't heard from Jack or from his stick-up-the-butt chief of staff. So when she walked into the reception area and didn't spot a familiar face, she wasn't surprised.

What did surprise her was how deep the disappointment went. She'd been so busy she hadn't had time to dwell on the confused feelings Jack Mason stirred in her. Except at night, when she dropped into bed exhausted and exhilarated and wishing she had someone to share the moments of her day with. Or when her body reminded her that she wasn't its sole inhabitant anymore. Or when she happened to spot a tall, tanned male across the room or on the street or in the subway.

"Don't be stupid," she muttered as she signed form after form. "He's making the world safer for our embassy people. That has to take precedence."

She was concentrating so fiercely on the clipboard in her hand that she didn't hear the door to the reception area open.

"Good, I'm not late."

The relieved exclamation brought her head up with a jerk. "Jack! I thought... Vickers said..."

Of all the idiotic times to get teary-eyed! How could she handle every crisis at work with a cheerful smile and turn into such a weepy wimp around this man? She had to jump off this emotional roller coaster.

"Vickers told me what he said." Grinning, he dropped into the chair beside hers. "He also told me what you said."

"Yes, well, you shouldn't piss off a preggo. The results aren't pretty."

"I'll remember that."

Guilt wormed through the simple, hedonistic pleasure of looking at his handsome face. She let the clipboard drop to her lap and made a wry face.

"You shouldn't have come. Vickers said you had a top-level conference going on all week."

"We wrapped up the last of the key issues this morning. All that's left is to approve the report once it gets drafted. I can do that by secure email. Which means," he said as he took the clipboard and flipped through the forms, "I don't have to fly back to D.C. right away. Here, you forgot to sign this one."

She scribbled her signature and tried not to read too much into his casual comment about extending his trip up from D.C. Didn't work. When he tacked on an equally casual invitation, her heart gave a little bump.

"If you don't have plans, I thought I might take you and the duchess to dinner tonight."

"Oh, I can't. I'm working a fiftieth anniversary party. I had to sneak out for this appointment."

"How about tomorrow?"

The bump was bigger this time. "Are you staying over that long?"

"Actually, I told Dale to clear the entire weekend."

"Ha! Bet he loved that."

"He's not so bad, Gina. You two just got off on the wrong foot."

"Wrong foot, wrong knee, wrong hip and elbow. How long has he worked for you, anyway?"

"Five years."

"And no one's ever told you he's officious or condescending?"

"No."

"It has to be me, then." Grimacing, she rolled out the reason she suspected might be behind his aide's less-than-enthusiastic response to her call. "Or the fact that the paparazzi will have a field day when they hear you knocked me up."

"They probably will," he replied, not quite suppressing a wince. "But when they do, you might want to use a different phrase to describe the circumstances."

"Really? What phrase do you suggest I use, Mr. Ambassador?"

He must have seen the chasm yawning at his feet. "Sorry. I didn't mean to come across as such a pompous jerk."

The apology soothed Gina's ruffled feathers enough for her to acknowledge his point. "I'm sorry, too. I know the pregnancy will cause you some embarrassment. I'll try not to add to it."

"The only embarrassing aspect to this whole situation is that I can't convince the beautiful and very stubborn mother of my child to marry me."

She wanted to believe him, but she wasn't that naive. She chewed on her lower lip for a moment before voicing the worry that had nagged her since Switzerland.

"Tell me the truth, Jack. Is this going to impact your career?"

"No."

"Maybe not at the State Department, but what about afterward? I read somewhere that certain powerful PACs think you have a good shot at the presidency in the not-too-distant future."

"Gina, listen to me." He curled a knuckle under her chin and tipped her face to make sure he had her complete attention. "We met, we were attracted to each other, we spent some time together. Since neither of us were then, or are now, otherwise committed, the only ones impacted by the result of that meeting are you, me and our baby."

"Wow," she breathed. "That was some speech, Mr. Ambassador. Those PACs may be right. You should make a bid for the Oval Office. You'd get my vote."

He feathered the side of her jaw with his thumb. "I'd rather get your signature on a marriage license."

Maybe…maybe she was being blind and pigheaded and all wrong about this marriage thing. So he didn't love her? He wanted her, and God knew she wanted him. Couldn't their child be the bridge to something more?

The thought made her cringe inside. What kind of mother would pile her hopes and dreams on a baby's tiny shoulders?

"We've had this discussion." Shrugging, she pulled away from his touch. "Let's not get into it again."

Surprise darkened his brown eyes, followed by a touch of what could have been either disappointment or irritation. Before Gina could decide which, a nurse in pink-and-blue scrubs decorated with storks delivering bundles of joy popped into the waiting room.

"Ms. St. Sebastian?"

"Right here."

"If you'll come with me, I'll get your height and weight and show you to an exam room."

Gina pushed out her chair. Jack rose with her. The nurse stopped him with a friendly smile. "Please wait here, Mr. St. Sebastian. I'll come get you in a few minutes."

The look on his face was more than enough to disperse Gina's glum thoughts. Choking back a laugh, she floated after the nurse. When Jack joined her in the exam room five minutes later, she was wearing a blue paper gown tied loosely in the front and a fat grin.

"I set her straight on the names."

"Uh-huh."

"Come on," she teased. "You have to admit it was funny."

The only thing in Jack's mind at the moment was not something he could admit. How could he have forgotten how full and lush and ripe her breasts were? Or had her pregnancy enhanced the creamy slopes he glimpsed through the front opening of her gown?

Whatever! That one glimpse was more than enough to put him in a sweat. Thoroughly disgusted, he was calling himself all kinds of a pig when the doctor walked in.

"Hello, Ms. St. Sebastian. I'm Dr. Martinson."

Petite and gray-haired, she shook hands with her patient before turning to Jack. "And you're Ambassador Mason, the baby's father?"

"That's right."

"I read through your medical and family histories. I'm so pleased neither of you smoke, use drugs, or drink to excess. That makes my job so much easier."

She included Jack in her approving smile before addressing Gina.

"I'm going to order lab tests to confirm your blood type and Rh status. We'll also check for anemia, syphilis, hepatitis B and the HIV virus, as well as your immunity to rubella and chicken pox. I want you to give a urine sample, as well."

Her down-to-earth manner put her patient instantly at ease…right up until the moment she extracted a pair of rubber gloves from a dispenser mounted on the wall.

"Let's get the pelvic exam out of the way, then we'll talk about what to expect in the next few weeks and months."

She must have caught the consternation that flooded into Gina's china blue eyes. Without missing a beat, the doc snapped on the gloves and issued a casual order.

"Why don't you wait outside, Ambassador Mason? This will only take a few moments."

Five

When Jack accompanied Gina out of the medical plaza complex and into the early throes of the Thursday evening rush hour, he was feeling a little shell-shocked.

The news that he would be a father had surprised the hell out of him initially. Once he'd recovered, he'd progressed in quick order from consternation to excitement to focusing his formidable energy on hustling the mother of his child to the altar. Now, with a copy of *A Father's Guide to Pregnancy* tucked in the pocket of his suit coat and the first prenatal behind him, he was beginning to appreciate both the reality and the enormity of the road ahead.

Gina, amazingly, seemed to be taking her pregnancy in stride. Like a gloriously painted butterfly, she'd gone through an almost complete metamorphosis. Not that she'd had much choice. With motherhood staring her in the face, she appeared to have shed her fun-loving, party-girl persona. The hysterical female who'd called Jack from Switzerland had also disappeared. Or maybe those personas had combined to produce this new Gina. Still bubbling with life, still gorgeous beyond words, but surprisingly responsible.

She'd listened attentively to everything the doctor said, asked obviously well-thought-out questions and made careful notes of the answers. She also worked the calendar on her iPhone with flying fingers to fit a visit to the lab for the required blood tests and future appointments with Dr. Martinson into her schedule.

In between, she fielded a series of what had sounded like frantic calls from work with assurances that yes, she'd confirmed delivery of the ice sculpture; no, their clients hadn't requested special permission from the New York City Department of Corrections for their grandson currently serving time at Rikers to attend their fiftieth wedding anniversary celebration; and yes, she'd just left the doctor's office and was about to jump in a cab.

Jack waited on the sidewalk beside her while she finished that last call. The sky was gray and overcast but the lack of sunshine didn't dim the luster of her hair. The tumble of shining curls and the buttercup-yellow tunic she wore over patterned yellow-and-turquoise tights made her a beacon of bright cheer in the dismal day.

Jack stood beside her, feeling a kick to the gut as he remembered exploring the lush curves under that bright tunic. Remembering, too, the kiss they'd shared the last time he put her in a cab. He'd spent more time trying to analyze his reaction to that kiss than he wanted to admit. It was hot and heavy on his mind when Gina finished her call.

"I have to run," she told him. "If you still want to take Grandmama and me to dinner, I could do tomorrow evening."

"That works."

"I'll check with her to make sure tomorrow's okay and give you a call."

He stepped to the curb and flagged a cab. She started to duck inside and hesitated.

Was she remembering the last time he'd put her in a cab, too? Jack's stomach went tight with the anticipation of taking her in his arms again. He'd actually taken a step forward when she issued a tentative invitation.

"Would you like to see where I work?"

The intensity of his disappointment surprised him, but he disguised it behind an easy smile. "Yeah, I would."

"It'll have to be a brief tour," she warned when they got in the cab. "We're in the final throes of an anniversary celebration with two hundred invited guests."

"Not including the grandson at Rikers."

She made a face. "Keep your fingers crossed he doesn't break out! I have visions of NYPD crashing through the doors just when we parade the cake."

"You parade cakes?"

"Sometimes. And in this instance, we'll do it very carefully! We're talking fifteen layers replicating the Cape Hatteras lighthouse that stands on the spot where our honorees got engaged."

She thumbed her iPhone and showed Jack an image of the iconic black-and-white striped lighthouse still guarding the shores of North Carolina's Outer Banks.

"We're doing an actual working model. The caterer and I had several sticky sessions before we figured out how to bury the battery pack in the cake base and power up the strobe light at the top without melting all his pretty sugar frosting into a black-and-white blob."

"I'm impressed."

And not just with the ingenuity and creativity she obviously brought to her new job. Enthusiasm sparkled in her blue eyes, and the vibrancy that had first snared his interest bubbled to the surface again.

"Hopefully, our clients will be impressed, too. We're decorating the entire venue in an Outer Banks theme. All sand, seashells and old boats, with enough fishnet and colorful buoys to supply the Atlantic fleet."

Unbidden and unwanted, a comparison surfaced between the woman beside him and the woman he'd loved with every atom of his being. The vivid images of Catherine were starting to fade, though, despite Jack's every effort to hang on to them. He had to dig deep to remember the sound of her laughter. Strain to hear an echo of her chuckle. She'd been so socially and politically involved. So serious about the issues that mattered to her. She had fun, certainly, but she hadn't regarded life as a frothy adventure the way Gina seemed to. Nor would she have rebounded so quickly from the emotional wringer of Switzerland.

As his companion continued her lighthearted description of tonight's event, Jack's memories of his wife retreated to the shadows once again. Even the shadows got blasted away when he and Gina exited the elevators onto the third floor of the Tremayne Group's midtown venue.

They could be on the Outer Banks, right at the edge of the Atlantic. Bemused, Jack took in the rolling sand dunes, the upended rowboat, the electronic waves splashing across a wall studded with LED lights.

"Wow. Is this all your doing?" he asked Gina.

"Not hardly. Mostly my boss, Samuel, and…uh-oh! There's Samuel now. He's with our big boss. 'Scuse me a minute. I'd better find out what's up."

Jack recognized the diminutive woman with the salt-and-pepper corkscrew curls at first look. Nicole Tremayne hadn't changed much in the past eight years. One of the underlings in her Boston operation had handled most of the planning for Jack's wedding to Catherine, but Nicole had approved the final plans herself and flown up from New York to personally oversee the lavish affair.

He saw the moment she recognized him, too. The casual glance she threw his way suddenly sharpened into a narrow-eyed stare. Frowning, she exchanged a few words with Gina, then crossed the floor.

"John Harris Mason." She thrust out a hand. "I should have made the connection when Gina demanded to know if Jack Mason had contacted me."

"I hope you told her no. She almost bit off my head when I offered to call and put in a word for her."

"She did? Interesting."

Chin cocked, Tremayne studied him through bird-bright eyes. She wasn't so crass as to come out and ask if he were the father of Gina's baby but Jack could see the speculation rife in her face.

"I was sorry to hear about your wife," she said after a moment.

"Thank you."

God, what a useless response. But Jack had uttered it so many times now that the words didn't taste quite as bitter in his mouth.

"Are you still in Boston?" she asked.

"No, I'm with the State Department now. Right now I'm assigned to D.C."

"Hmm." She tapped a bloodred nail against her chin. "Good to know."

With that enigmatic comment she excused herself and returned to her underlings. Gina rushed over a few moments later.

"I'm so sorry, Jack. We'll have to postpone the tour. I've got to take care of an ice-sculpture crisis."

"No problem. Just let me know if tomorrow evening's a go for the duchess."

"I will."

The following evening was not only a go, but the duchess's acceptance also came with an invitation for drinks at the Dakota prior to dinner.

Jack spent all that day at the NYPD Counterterrorism Bureau established after 9/11. While coordination between federal, state and local agencies had increased exponentially since that horrific day, there was always room for improvement. The NYPD agents were particularly interested in Jack's recent up-close-and-personal encounter with a rabidly anti-U.S. terrorist cell in Mali. They soaked up every detail of the terrorists' weaponry and tactics and poured over the backgrounds of two Americans recently ID'd as part of the group. Since the parents of one of the expatriates lived in Brooklyn, NYPD was justifiably worried that the son might try to slip back into the country.

Jack in turn received in-depth briefings on the Counterterrorism Bureau's Lower Manhattan Security Initiative. Designed to protect the nation's financial capital, the LMSI combined increased police presence and the latest surveillance technology with a public-private partnership. Individuals from both government and the business world manned LMSI's operations center to detect and neutralize potential threats. Jack left grimly hopeful that this unique public-private cooperative effort would prove a model for other high-risk targets.

He rushed back to his hotel and had his driver wait while he hurried upstairs to change his shirt and eliminate his five-o'clock shadow. A half hour later he identified himself to a uniformed doorman at the castlelike Dakota. The security at the famed apartment complex had stepped up considerably after one of its most famous tenants, John Lennon, was gunned down just steps away from the entrance years ago. Jack had no problem providing identification, being closely scrutinized and waiting patiently while the doorman called upstairs.

"The duchess is expecting you, sir. You know the apartment number?"

"I do."

"Very good." He keyed a remote to unlock the inner door. "The elevators are to your left."

A dark-haired, generously endowed woman Jack remembered from the wedding reception answered the doorbell. She wore a polite expression but he sensed disapproval lurking just below the surface.

"*Hola.* I am Maria, housekeeper to *la duquesa* and auntie to Sarah and Gina."

Auntie, huh? That explained the disapproval. She obviously considered him solely responsible for the failure of the box of condoms he and Gina had gone through during their sexual extravaganza.

"Good evening, Maria. I saw you at Sarah's wedding but didn't get a chance to introduce myself. I'm Jack Mason."

"*Sí,* I know. Please come with me. *La duquesa* waits for you in the salon."

He followed her down a hall tiled in pale pink Carrara marble. The delicate scent of orange blossoms wafted from a Waterford crystal bowl set on a rococo side table. The elegant accessories gave no hint of how close the duchess had come to financial disaster. Jack picked up faint traces of it, however, when Maria showed him into the high-ceilinged salon.

The room's inlaid parquet floor was a work of art but cried for a hand-knotted Turkish carpet to soften its hard surface. Likewise, the watered silk wallpaper showed several barely discernible lighter rectangles where paintings must have once hung. The furniture was a skillful blend of fine antiques and modern comfort, though, and the floor-to-ceiling windows curtained in pale blue velvet gave glorious views of Central Park. Those swift impressions faded into insignificance when Jack spotted the woman sitting ramrod-straight in a leather-backed armchair, her cane within easy reach. Thin and frail though she was, Charlotte St. Sebastian nevertheless dominated the salon with her regal air.

"Good evening, Jack."

She held out a veined hand. He shook it gently and remembered her suggestion at the wedding that he use her name instead of her title.

"Good evening, Charlotte."

"Gina called a few moments ago. She's been detained at work but should be here shortly."

She waved him to the chair beside hers and smiled a request at Maria. "Would you bring in the appetizer tray before you leave?"

When the housekeeper bustled out, the duchess gestured

to a side table holding a dew-streaked bucket and an impressive array of crystal decanters.

"May I offer you an aperitif?"

"You may."

"I'm afraid I must ask you to serve yourself. The wine is a particularly fine French white, although some people find the Aligoté grape a bit too light for their tastes. Or…"

She lifted the tiny liqueur glass sitting on the table next to her and swirled its amber liquid.

"You may want to try *žuta osa*. It's produced in the mountains that at one time were part of the Duchy of Karlenburgh."

The bland comment didn't fool Jack for a second. He'd responded to too many toasts by foreign dignitaries and downed too many potent local brews to trust this one. He poured a glass of wine instead.

Maria returned with a silver tray containing a selection of cheeses, olives and prosciutto ham slices wrapped around pale green melon slices. She placed the tray on a massive marble-topped coffee table within easy reach of the duchess and her guest.

"Thank you." Charlotte gave her a smile composed of equal parts gratitude and affection. "You'd better leave now. You don't want to miss your bus."

"I'll take a later one."

Her quick glance in Jack's direction said she wasn't about to leave her friend and employer in his clutches. The duchess didn't miss the suspicion in her dark eyes.

"We're fine," she assured the woman. "Go ahead and catch your bus."

Maria looked as though she wanted to dig in her heels but yielded to her employer's wishes. The kitchen door swished shut behind her. Several moments later, her heavy footsteps sounded in the hall.

"Actually," Jack said when he resumed his seat beside the duchess, "I'm glad we have some time alone."

"Indeed?"

"As you know, Gina and I didn't spend all that much time together before our lives became so inextricably linked."

"I am aware of that fact."

Deciding he'd be wise to ignore the pained expression on Charlotte's face, Jack pressed ahead. "I'm just beginning to appreciate the woman behind your granddaughter's dazzlingly beautiful exterior. I'm hoping you'll help me add to that portrait by telling me a little more about her."

One aristocratic brow lifted. "Surely you don't expect me to provide ammunition for your campaign to convince Gina to marry you?"

"As a matter of fact, that's exactly what I'm hoping you'll provide."

"Well!" The brow shot up another notch. "For a career diplomat, you're very frank."

"I've found being frank works better than tiptoeing around tough issues."

"And that's how you categorize my granddaughter?" the duchess said haughtily. "A tough issue?"

"Ha!" Jack didn't bother to disguise his feelings. "Tough doesn't even begin to describe her. To put it bluntly, your granddaughter is the toughest, stubbornest, most irritating issue I've ever dealt with."

Oh, hell. The frozen look on his hostess's face said clearer than words that he'd overshot his mark. He was just about to apologize profusely when the facade cracked and the duchess broke into somewhat less than regal snorts of laughter.

"You do know," she responded some moments later, "that Gina says exactly the same thing about you?"

"Yes, ma'am, I do."

Still chuckling, she lifted her glass and tossed back the remainder of the amber liquid.

"Shall I pour you another?" Jack asked.

"Thank you, no. My doctor insists I limit myself to one a day. He's a fussy old woman, but he's kept me alive this long so I suppose I can't complain. Now, what do you want to know about Gina?"

Feeling as though he'd managed to negotiate a particularly dangerous minefield, Jack relaxed. "Whatever you feel comfortable sharing. Maybe you could start when she was a child. What kind of mischief did she get into?"

"Good heavens! What kind didn't she get into?" A fond smile lit the duchess's clouded blue eyes. "I remember one incident in particular. She couldn't have been more than seven or eight at the time. Maria had taken her and Sarah to the park. Gina wandered off and threw us all into a state of complete panic. The police were searching for her when she showed up several hours later with a lice-infested baglady in tow. She'd found the woman asleep under a bush and simply couldn't leave her on the cold, hard ground. I believe the woman stayed with us for almost a week before Gina was satisfied with the arrangements we worked out for her."

Charlotte's wry tale added another piece to the mosaic that was Gina St. Sebastian. Jack was trying to assemble the varied and very different sections into a coherent whole when the front door slammed.

"It's me, Grandmama. Is Jack here yet?"

The question was accompanied by the thud of something heavy hitting the table in the hall. Wincing, the duchess called out an answer.

"He is. We're in the salon."

With a kick in his pulse, Jack rose to greet her. His welcoming smile faltered and came close to falling off his face when she waltzed into the salon.

"Sorry I'm late."

"Eugenia!" the duchess gasped. "Your hair!"

"Pretty, isn't it?" Gina patted her ruler-straight, bright purple locks and shot her grandmother a mischievous grin. "We're doing a manga-themed birthday party tomorrow afternoon. I'm Yuu Nomiya."

"I don't have the faintest idea who manga or Yuu are, but I sincerely hope that color isn't permanent."

"It'll come out after a few washings." With that blithe assurance, she gave Jack an apologetic smile. "I'm sorry I kept you waiting. We haven't missed our dinner reservation, have we?"

"We've plenty of time." He struggled to keep his eyes on her face and off the neon purple framing it. "Would you like something to drink? I'm doing the honors."

"God, yes!"

She dropped onto the sofa in an untidy sprawl and caught the suddenly disapproving expressions on the two faces turned in her direction.

"What? Oh! I don't want anything alcoholic. Just tonic, with lots of ice."

Jack delivered the tonic and listened while Gina tried to explain the concept of Japanese manga comics to her grandmother. In the process, she devoured most of the contents of the appetizer tray.

To her credit, the duchess appeared genuinely curious about the phenomenon now taking the world by storm. Or perhaps she just displayed an interest for her granddaughter's sake. Whatever the reason, she asked a series of very intelligent questions. Gina answered them with enthusiasm…at first. Gradually, her answers grew shorter and more muddled. At the same time she slipped lower against the sofa cushions. When her lids drooped and she lost her train of thought in midsentence, the duchess sighed.

"Eugenia, my darling. You're exhausted. Go to bed."

The order fell on deaf ears. Her granddaughter was out like a light.

"I warned her," Charlotte said with affectionate exasperation. "The first few months especially sap a woman's strength."

"Dr. Martinson said the same thing."

"We'll have to forego dinner, Jack. She needs to rest."

"Of course."

When the duchess grasped her cane and aimed the tip at her sleeping granddaughter, he pushed out of his chair.

"Don't wake her."

Bending, he eased her into his arms. She muttered something unintelligible and snuggled against his chest. The scent and the feel of her tantalized Jack's senses. His throat tightening, he growled out a request for directions.

"Which way is her bedroom?"

Six

Gina was having the best dream. She was cradled in strong arms, held against a warm, hard chest. She felt so safe, so secure. So treasured. Like something precious and fragile, which even in her dream she knew she wasn't. Savoring the sensation of being sheltered and protected, she ignored a pesky pressure low in her belly and nuzzled her nose into something soft and squeezy.

The soft and squeezy, her hazy mind determined a moment later, was her pillow. And that irritating pressure was her bladder demanding relief. She pried up an eyelid and made out the dim outlines of her bedroom. The faint glow of the night-light always left on showed she was tucked under the satin throw she normally kept folded at the foot of the bed. She was also fully dressed.

Grunting, she got an elbow under her and sat up. Her slept-in clothes felt scratchy and twisted and tight. Long strands of purple hair fell across her eyes. She brushed them back and tossed aside the throw. Still groggy, she made her way to the bathroom. Once back in the bedroom she shed her clothes and slid into bed, between the sheets this time.

Sleep tugged at her. She drifted toward it on the vague

remnants of her dream. Those strong arms… That steady pulse of a heartbeat under her cheek…

"Jack?"

She sat up again, suddenly and fully awake, and flipped onto her other hip. The covers on the other side of the bed lay smooth and flat. Intense and totally absurd disappointment made her scrunch her face in disgust.

"Idiot! Like the man's going to crawl into bed with you? Right here, in the apartment? And Grandmama only a snore away?"

She flopped back down and yanked the sheet up to her chin. In almost the next breath, her disappointment took a sharp right turn into thigh-clenching need. The hunger shot straight from her breasts to her belly. From there it surged to every extremity, until even her fingernails itched with it.

She stared at the ceiling, her breath coming hot and fast. Images fast-forwarded in her mind. Jack leaning over her, his muscles slick and taunt. Jack laughing as she rolled him onto his back and straddled him. Jack's hands splayed on her naked hips and his jaw tight while he rose up to meet her downward thrust.

Oh, man! She should have expected this. One of the pamphlets Dr. Martinson had provided specifically addressed the issue of heightened sex drive during pregnancy. The rampaging hormones, the supersensitive breasts, the increased blood supply to the vulva— Taken together they could brew up a perfect storm of insatiable physical hunger.

Gina was there. Smack in the eye of the storm. She ached for Jack. She wanted him on her and in her and…

"Oh, for Pete's sake!"

Throwing off the sheet, she stalked to the antique dressing table with its tri-fold mirror, marble top and dozens of tiny drawers. She couldn't begin to count the number of hours she'd spent at this table. First as a youngster playing dress-up in Grandmama's pearls and Sarah's lacy peignoir. Then as a preteen, giggling with her girlfriends while they pirouetted in panties and training bras to show off their budding figures. After that came the high school years of mascara and eye shadow and love notes and trinkets from a steady stream of boys drooling over her nicely filled-out curves.

The notes and trinkets were long gone but her trusty vibrator was tucked in its usual drawer. She didn't have to resort to it often, but this…this gnawing hunger constituted a medical emergency.

So much of an emergency that the relief was almost instantaneous. And too damned short-lived! Gina tried to go from limp and languid into sleep. Jack kept getting in the way. Had he been bummed about dinner? Did he and Grandmama go without her? Would he try to see her again before he flew back to Washington?

She was forced to wait for the answers to those questions. With the manga birthday party set to kick off at 11:00 a.m., she had to leave for work before the duchess emerged from her bedroom. Maria came in at midmorning on Saturdays so Gina got no help from that quarter, either.

She toyed with the idea of calling Jack during the short subway ride to midtown, but all-too-vivid memories of last night's searing hunger kept her cell phone in her purse. The memories raised heat in her cheeks. She suspected that hearing his voice, all deep and rich, would produce even more graphic effects. She wasn't showing up for work with her nipples threatening to poke through bra and blouse.

That didn't stop said nipples from sitting up and taking notice, however, when Jack contacted her just after nine-thirty.

"How are you doing, sleepyhead?"

"Better this morning than last night." Jamming the phone between her chin and shoulder, she initialed the final seating plan and handed it to Kallie to add table numbers to name tags. "Sorry I zonked out on you."

"No problem. The duchess didn't want to leave you, so we ordered in."

"Corned beef on rye from Osterman's, right?"

"How did you know?"

"That's what we usually order in."

"We had a nice, long talk while we ate, by the way."

"Uh-oh! Did she leave any stones from my misspent youth unturned?"

"One or two. She said you'll have to turn over the rest yourself. She also said she was meeting with her opera club this evening. So that leaves just us. We can do a make-up dinner. Unless you have to work…"

He'd left her an easy out. It said much for Gina's state of mind that she didn't even consider taking it.

"I'm doing the party kickoff but Samuel's taking cleanup. I should be done here by three."

"I'll pick you up then."

"Kind of early for dinner," she commented.

"We'll find something to do."

His breezy confidence took a hit when she slid into the cab he drove up in. Groaning, she let her purpled head drop onto the seat back.

"Next time I tell you I'm helping with a birthday party for a slew of eight- and nine-year-olds, be kind. Just shoot me right between the eyes."

"That bad, huh?"

"Worse."

"Guess that means you're not up for a stroll down Fifth Avenue."

"Do I look like I'm up for a stroll?"

"Well…"

She angled her head and studied him through a thick screen of purple-tipped lashes. "You, bastard that you are, appear relaxed and refreshed and disgustingly up for anything."

Jack laughed and decided not to bore her with the details of his day, which had kicked off at 4:32 a.m. with a call from the State Department's twenty-four-hour crisis monitoring desk. They reported that an angry crowd had gathered at the U.S. Embassy in Islamabad, and a debate was raging within the department over whether to reinforce the marine guard by flying in a fleet antiterrorist security team. Thankfully, the crowd dispersed with no shots fired and no FAST team required, but Jack had spent the rest of the morning and early afternoon reading the message traffic and analyzing the flash points that had precipitated the seemingly spontaneous mob.

Although the crisis had been averted, Jack knew he should have jumped a shuttle and flown back to D.C. His decision to remain in New York another night had surprised him almost as it had his chief of staff, Dale Vickers.

Jack had first met Dale at Harvard, when they both were enrolled in the Kennedy School of Government. Like Jack, Dale had also gone into the Foreign Service and had spent almost a decade in the field as a Foreign Service Officer until increasingly severe bouts of asthma chained him to a desk at State Department headquarters. *Chained* being the operative word. Unmarried and fiercely dedicated, Vickers spent fourteen to sixteen hours a day, every day, at his desk.

Jack appreciated his second-in-command's devotion. He didn't appreciate the disdain that crept into Vickers's voice after learning his boss intended to stay another night in New York.

"We've kept your relationship with Ms. St. Sebastian out of the press so far, Ambassador. I'm not sure how much longer we can continue to do so."

"Don't worry about it. I don't."

"Easy for you to say," Dale sniffed, displaying the prissy side he didn't even suspect he possessed. "Media relations is my job."

"I repeat, don't worry about it. If and when the story breaks, Ms. St. Sebastian and I will handle it."

That was met with a short, charged silence. Jack had worked with Vickers long enough now to know there was more to come. It came slowly, with seeming reluctance.

"You might want to discuss the slant we should give Ms. Sebastian's pregnancy with your father, Ambassador. He expressed some rather strong views on the matter when he called here and I told him you were in New York."

"First," Jack said coldly, "I don't want you discussing my personal affairs with anyone, including my father. Second, there is no slant. Gina St. Sebastian is pregnant with my child. What happens next is our business. Not the media's. Not the State Department's. Not my father's. Not yours. Got that?"

"Yes, sir."

"Good. I'll let you know when I book the return shuttle to D.C."

Fragments of that conversation played in Jack's mind now as he studied the purple-tipped lashes framing Gina's eyes. When his gaze drifted from those purple tips to her hair, he found himself repressing an inner qualm at the prospect of bumping into some member of the paparazzi. Jack could only imagine his father's reaction to seeing Gina splashed across the tabloids in her manga persona.

John Harris II still mourned Catherine's death but in recent years he'd turned his energy to finding a suitable replacement. Preferably someone with his daughter-in-law's family wealth and political connections. He would accept an outsider if pushed to the edge. But Gina...?

"What are you thinking?" she asked, yanking Jack back to the present.

Everything fell away except the woman next to him. He relaxed into a lazy sprawl, his thighs and hips matched with hers. "I'm thinking I skipped lunch. How about you? Did you scarf down whatever you ordered up for that slew of eight-and nine-year-olds?"

"Puh-leez." Her shoulders quivered in an exaggerated shudder. "My system can only take so much sugar."

Her system, and her baby.

Only now did Gina appreciate the 180-degree turn her diet had taken. She'd cut out all forms of alcohol the moment she'd suspected she was pregnant. After her initial appointment with Dr. Martinson, she'd also cut out caffeine and started tossing down neonatal vitamins brimming with iron and folic acid. She hadn't experienced any middle-of-the-night cravings yet but suddenly, inexplicably, she had to have a foot-long smothered in sauerkraut.

"How does a picnic sound?" she asked. "One of my favorite street vendors works a corner close to Bryant Park. We could grab a couple of fat, juicy hot dogs and do some serious people watching."

"I'm game."

Bryant Park encapsulated everything Gina loved about New York. Located between 5th and 6th Avenues and bounded on the eastern side by the New York Public Library, it formed an island of leafy green amid an ocean of skyscrapers. On weekdays office workers crowded the park's benches or stretched out on the lawn during their lunch hours. If they had the time and the ambition, they could also sign up for a Ping-Pong game or backgammon or a chess match. Out-of-towners, too, were drawn to the park's gaily painted carousel, the free concerts, the movies under the stars and, glory of glory, the superclean public restrooms. Chattering in a dozen different languages, tourists wandered the glassed-in kiosks or collapsed at tables in the outdoor restaurant to take a breather from determined sightseeing.

This late in the afternoon Gina and Jack could have snagged a table at the Bryant Park Grill or the more informal café. She was a woman on a mission, however. Leaning forward, she instructed the cab driver to cruise a little way past the park and kept her eyes peeled for an aluminum-sided cart topped by a bright yellow umbrella.

"There he is. Pull over."

Mere moments later she and Jack carried their soft drinks and foil-wrapped treasures into the park. Gina had ordered hers doused with a double helping of sauerkraut. Jack had gone the more conservative mustard-and-relish route. The scent had her salivating until they snagged an empty bench.

"Oh, God," Gina moaned after the first bite. "This is almost better than sex."

Jack cocked a brow and paused with his dog halfway to his mouth.

"I said 'almost.'"

If she'd had a grain of common sense, she would have left it there. But, no. Like an idiot, she had to let her mouth run away with her.

"Not that I've had anything to compare it to in the past couple of months," she mumbled around another bite.

"We can fix that."

Jack tossed the words out so easily, so casually, that it took a second or two for his meaning to register. When it did, Gina choked on the bite she'd just taken.

"I've been doing my assigned reading," he said as he gave her a helpful thump on the back. "*A Father's Guide to Pregnancy* says it's not uncommon for a woman's libido to shoot into the stratosphere, particularly during the first trimester. It also warned me not to feel inadequate if I don't satisfy what could turn into an insatiable appetite."

He didn't look all that concerned about the possibility. Just the opposite. The wicked glint in his brown eyes positively challenged Gina to give him a shot.

She wanted to. God, she wanted to! Just looking at his beautiful mouth with a tiny smear of mustard at the corner made her ache to lean in and lick it off. She had to gulp down a long slug of Sprite Zero to keep from giving in to the impulse.

"I appreciate the offer," she said with what she hoped was a cheeky smile. "I'll keep it in mind if I run out of batteries."

"Ouch."

He put on a good show of being wounded, but when the laughter faded from his eyes she saw the utter seriousness in their depths.

"I know you want a relationship based on more than just sex, Gina. I'm hoping we can build that partnership."

"I know you are."

"We're not there yet," he admitted with brutal honesty, "but we're getting closer."

Ha! He could speak for himself. She was standing right on the edge, and every moment she spent with this man cut more ground from under her feet. All it would take was one gentle push. She'd fall for him so fast he wouldn't know what hit him.

Unfortunately, everything else would fall with her. Her fledgling career. Her self-respect. Her pride. She was just starting to feel good about herself. Just beginning to believe she could be the responsible parent she wanted so desperately to become.

Oh, hell! Who was she kidding? She would dump it all in a heartbeat if Jack loved her.

But he didn't. Yet.

So she wouldn't. Yet.

Consoled by the possibilities embedded in that little three-letter word, she tried to keep it light. "Too bad this isn't horseshoes. We would score points for close. Let's just…let's just press on the way we have been and hope for a ringer."

Stupid metaphor but the best she could come up with at the moment. Jack looked as if he wanted to say more but let it go. They sat knee-to-knee in the sunshine and devoured their hot dogs. Or more correctly, Gina devoured hers. Jack had set his on the unwrapped foil to pop the top of his soft drink. He took a long swig and rested the can on his knee while he watched two twentysomethings duking it out at the Ping-Pong table. The crack of their paddles smacking the ball formed a sharp counterpoint to the carousel's merry tune and the traffic humming along 6th Avenue.

"This is nice," Jack commented. "I don't get to just sit and bask in the sun much anymore."

"Uh-huh."

He stretched an arm along the back of the bench. "Did you come here often when you were growing up?"

"Yep."

Her abbreviated responses brought his gaze swinging back to her just in time to catch the covetous looks she was giving his not-yet-consumed weenie. She didn't bother to plead innocence.

"Are you going to eat that?"

"It's all yours. Or shall I go get you another one doused with sauerkraut?"

She gave the question serious consideration before shaking her head. "This will do me."

The remains disappeared in two bites. Semi-satisfied, Gina leaned against the bench and stretched out her legs. His arm formed a comfortable backrest as she replied to his earlier query.

"I couldn't even hazard a guess how many times I've been to Bryant Park. Maria used to bring Sarah and me to ride the merry-go-round or ice-skate on Citi Pond. Grandmama would come, too, after shopping on Fifth Avenue or to wait while we girls hit the library."

"Your grandmother's a remarkable woman."

"Yes, she is."

"Are she and Sarah the only family you have left?"

"There are some distant cousins in Slovenia. Or maybe it's Hungary. Or Austria. To tell the truth, I'm not real sure which countries got which parts of Karlenburgh after the duchy was broken up."

"Has Charlotte ever gone back?"

"No, never. She doesn't say so, but I know it would be too painful for her."

"What about you?" He toyed with the ends of her hair, still straight, still purple. "Have you ever visited your ancestral lands?"

"Not yet. I'd like to, though. One of these days…"

She could sit here for hours, she thought lazily. Listening to the crack of the Ping-Pong paddles, watching the tourists nose through the kiosks, nestling her head on the solid heat of Jack's arm. She didn't realize her eyelids had fluttered shut until his amused voice drifted down to her.

"You going to sleep on me again?"

"Maybe."

"Before you zone out completely, let's set a date for you to make a visit to D.C. My folks are anxious to meet you."

That woke her up. The little she knew about Jack's family suggested they probably wouldn't welcome her with open arms. Not his father, anyway. But she'd promised. Digging into her purse, she checked the calendar on her iPhone.

"I can't do next weekend. Does the second weekend in June work for you?"

"I'll make it work. Go back to sleep now."

Seven

Gina ended up making the jaunt down to Washington a week earlier than expected. Her change of plans kicked off the following Thursday morning with a summons to Samuel's office, where her boss relayed a request from the head office.

"Nicole just called. She needs you to fly down to D.C. You've got a reservation on the two-twenty shuttle."

"Today?"

"Yes, today. TTG's coordinating a black-tie reception and private, prerelease movie showing for two hundred tomorrow evening."

"And Elaine needs help?"

Elaine Patterson managed the TTG's Washington venue. Gina had met the trim, elegant brunette once when she'd flown to New York for a meeting with Samuel.

"Elaine's father had a heart attack. She's in Oregon and her assistant just checked into the ICU with a bad case of pancreatitis, whatever the hell that is. The rest of the staff is too junior to handle a function this large. Nicole wants you to take charge."

Samuel shoved a folder across his desk. "Here are faxed copies of the timetable, menu, floor plans, proposed setup, list of suppliers and contact phone numbers. I had them also email copies so you'll be able pull 'em on your iPad in case you need to make changes on the fly. You can stay in the venue's bridal suite. It's fully equipped and stocked."

"But…"

"I'll cover the consult you have scheduled for this afternoon."

"What about the Hanrahan retirement party on Saturday? I'm lead on that."

"I scanned the file. From the looks of the checklist, you've got everything in good shape. I'll take care of the last few prep tasks and get Kallie to pull floor duty with me."

Gina thought fast. She'd have to call Maria to see whether she could come in Sunday and check on Grandmama. If she could, Gina might extend her stay in D.C. for another day, possibly two.

The prospect of spending those days with Jack made her heart do its own version of a happy dance. She could feel it skittering and skipping as she let drop a casual comment.

"My calendar's pretty light on Monday. I don't have anything scheduled that can't be moved. I may take some comp time and stay over in Washington."

"Fine by me." He flapped a hand. "Just get your butt in gear."

She got her butt in gear!

A call made while the cab whisked her uptown confirmed Maria would be happy to check on *la duquesa* Sunday afternoon. When Gina dashed in and explained the arrangement, Grandmama issued an indignant protest.

"I'm neither crippled nor incapacitated, Eugenia. There's no need for Maria to come all the way in to check on me."

"She's not doing it for you, she's doing it for me."

"Really," the duchess huffed. "It's not necessary."

"I know. Just humor me, okay? The thing is, I may stay

over in D.C. a day or two. Jack wants me to meet his parents. If they're available, I'll try to cram in a visit."

"Indeed?"

That bit of news stifled any further objections from her grandmother. Her faded blue eyes lingered thoughtfully on Gina's face for a moment before she commented dryly, "How fortunate the purple washed out of your hair."

Extremely fortunate, Gina thought as she rushed into the bedroom. She hurried out again after stuffing toiletries, a sequined tuxedo jacket she appropriated from Sarah's closet, black satin palazzo pants and some casual clothes into a weekender.

"I'll call you," she promised, dropping a kiss on her grandmother's cheek.

She hit the lobby and had Jerome flag her a cab to La-Guardia. Collapsing in the backseat, she fished out her phone and called Jack. His cell phone went to voice mail, so she left a quick message. For added insurance, she called his office and got shuffled to his chief of staff. Her nose wrinkling, she asked Vickers to advise his boss that she was flying down to Washington.

"Certainly, Ms. St. Sebastian."

He sounded a little more polite but about a mile and half from friendly. Gina wanted to ask him what his problem was but she suspected she already knew the answer.

She made her flight with all of five minutes to spare. When the adrenaline rush subsided and the plane lifted off, she rested her head against the seat back. The next thing she knew, the flight attendant was announcing their imminent arrival at Ronald Reagan National Airport. Gina blinked the sleep out of her eyes and enjoyed her view through the window of the capital's marble monuments.

The short nap left her energized and eager to plunge into the task ahead. She wheeled her weekender through the airport with a spring in her step and exited into a beautiful June day only slightly tainted by the exhaust pluming out of the cars and taxis and shuttles lined up outside the terminal.

Gina didn't have to dig deep to know why she was so jazzed. The idea that Nicole trusted her enough to step in at the last minute and take charge of a major event had given her self-confidence a shot in the arm.

Then there was the chance she might cram in some time with Jack. That possibility prodded her to whip out her cell phone and take it off airplane mode. The flashing icon indicating a text from Jack put a smile on her lips.

Just heard you're en route to D.C. Call when you arrive.

She crossed the street to the parking garage and aimed for the rental car area while she tried his private number. He answered on the second ring.

"You're here?"

The sound of his voice moved the smile from her lips to her heart. "I'm here. Just got in."

"This is a surprise. What brought you to D.C.?"

For once she managed to catch herself before blurting out the truth. He didn't need to know the possibility of spending some time with him was one of the reasons—the main reason—she'd jumped at this job.

"I'm a last-minute stand-in to coordinate an event tomorrow night."

"Which event?"

"A fancy-schmancy cocktail party and prerelease showing of the new action flick starring Dirk West."

Gina wasn't a real fan of the shoot-'em-up, blow-'em-up type movies West had been making for several decades but she knew every new release pulled in millions.

"The event's being hosted by Global Protective Services," she told Jack. "According to their company propaganda, they're—"

"One of the largest private security contractors in the

world," he interrupted. "They have more boots on the ground in Afghanistan right now than the U.S. military. Rumor is they put up most of the money for the movie. Probably because the script makes a very unsubtle case for decreasing the size of our standing armies and increasing the use of private mercenaries."

Holding the phone to her ear, Gina skimmed the Hertz reservation board to find the parking slot for the car Kallie said would be waiting for her.

"Sounds like this shindig would be right up your alley," she commented as she started down the long row of parked vehicles, "but I didn't see your name on the attendee list."

"That's because I declined the invitation. I might have to rethink that, though, if you're going to be working the event."

"Oh, sure," she said with a laugh. "Screw up the head count, why don't you?"

"I won't eat much," he promised solemnly.

"Well…" She found her car and tossed her briefcase onto the passenger seat. "I guess I can add you to the list."

"That takes care of tomorrow, then. What's on your agenda tonight?"

"I've got what's left of the TTG crew standing by." She slid into the driver's seat but waited to key the ignition. "We're going to go over the final task list and walk through the venue."

"How long will that take?"

"I have no idea."

She hesitated a moment before laying the possibility of an extended stay on him. Would she really be up to meeting his parents after working this event? Yes, dammit, she would.

"I told Samuel I might take a couple extra days in D.C. If it fits with your schedule and theirs, maybe we could work in a visit with your folks."

"We'll make it fit. I'll give them a call and arrange a time. Where are you staying?"

"At TTG's L'Enfant Plaza venue. We have a full bridal suite on the top floor."

"A bridal suite, huh?" His voice dropped to a slow, warm caress. "Want some company?"

God, yes! She gripped the phone, almost groaning at the idea of rolling around with Jack on the Tremayne Group's signature chocolate-brown sheets. Instant, erotic images of their bodies all sweaty and naked buzzed in her head like a swarm of pesky flies.

"Thanks for the offer," she said, making a valiant attempt to bat away the flies, "but I'd better pass."

Somewhat to her disappointment Jack didn't press the issue.

"You sure you can't sneak away for an hour or two and have dinner with me?" he asked instead.

Desire waged a fierce, no-holds-barred, free-for-all with duty. The old, fun-loving Gina would have yielded without a second thought. The new, still fun-loving but not quite as irresponsible Gina sighed.

"Sorry, Jack. I really need to spend this afternoon and evening prepping for the event."

He conceded with his usual easy charm. "I understand. I'll see you tomorrow."

Jack disconnected, swung his desk chair around and settled his gaze on the slice of Washington visible from his third-floor office. Since he held ambassadorial rank, he rated a full suite at the State Department's main headquarters on C Street.

The thirties-era building was originally designed to house the War Department, but the war planners outgrew it before it was completed. When they moved into the Pentagon in 1941, State inherited this massive structure constructed of buff-colored sandstone. It and its more modern annexes were located in the area of D.C. known as Foggy Bottom, so named because this section of the city was once a dismal, gray-misted swamp. Many of the talking heads who filled today's airwaves with their dubious wisdom liked to suggest the decisions coming out State were still pretty foggy and swampy.

The windows in Jack's office gave a narrow view down 21st Street to the National Mall, with the Lincoln Memorial at one end and the Washington Monument at the other. On good days he could almost catch the glitter of sunlight bouncing off the reflecting pool. The view didn't hold a particle of interest at the moment.

All his thoughts centered on Gina. The news that she was coming to Washington had proved the only bright spark in an otherwise grim morning spent reviewing casualty reports and incident analyses from twenty years of attacks on U.S. diplomatic outposts. Just the sound of her voice and merry laugh lightened his mood.

Thoughtfully, Jack tipped back his chair. Simply knowing that Gina was here, on his home turf, sparked a need that dug into him with sharp, fierce claws. Her image was etched in his mind. Those bright blue eyes. That luscious mouth. The tumble of white-blond curls.

The image shifted, and he pictured her manga'ed mane. God, what if she was still sporting that look? He could only imagine his father's reaction. The thought produced a wry grin as he swung his chair around and dialed his parents' number.

Jack brought his tux in to the office with him the next morning and changed before leaving work that evening. Anxious to see Gina, he arrived at L'Enfant Plaza early.

The plaza was named for Pierre Charles L'Enfant, the French-born architect recruited by General LaFayette to serve as an engineer with George Washington's Continental army. A long rectangle, the plaza was bordered on three sides by an amalgamation of office buildings, government agencies, retail shops and hotels. One of I. M. Pei's iconic glass pyramids dominated the center. A sister to the pyramid in front of the Louvre, it rose from a lower level with gleaming majesty.

The spot was a good choice for evening events. Foot and vehicle traffic died out when the surrounding offices emptied, leaving plenty of underground parking for guests. Or they could hop off the Metro and let the escalators whisk them up to the plaza. Jack had opted for plan B and emerged from the Metro's subterranean levels into a balmy June evening. Tiny white lights illuminated the trees lining two sides of the plaza. Centered between those sparkling rows, the lighted pyramid formed a dramatic backdrop for lavishly filled buffet tables and strategically placed carving stations.

Two dozen or so other early arrivals grazed the tables or clumped together in small groups with drinks in hand. Jack took advantage of the sparse crowd and lack of lines to hit one of the S-shaped bars set up close to the pyramid. He kept an eye out for Gina as he crossed the plaza but didn't spot either her blond curls or a waterfall of purple. Nor did he find a bartender behind the ebony-and-glass counter. He angled around to check the other bars and saw an attendant at only one. Flipping and tipping bottles, the harried attendant splashed booze and mixers into an array of glasses and shoved them at the tuxedoed waitstaff standing in line at his station.

The fact that three of the four bars weren't ready for action surprised Jack until he spotted Gina, a male in a white shirt and black vest and a plump female with a radio clipped to her waist hurrying out onto the plaza. The man peeled off in the direction of one unattended bar, the woman aimed for another. Gina herself edged behind the ebony S where Jack stood.

"Shorthanded?" he asked as she whipped bottles of champagne out of a refrigerated case and lined them up on the bar.

She rolled her eyes. "Just a tad."

When she started to attack the foil caps, he moved behind the bar to help. She flashed him a grateful look and set him to popping corks while she extracted champagne flutes from a rack beneath the counter.

"I should be in the media center making a last check of the seating," she told him, "but I've been on the phone with the bar subcontractor for twenty friggin' minutes. He's supposed to be sending replacements for their no-shows. You can bet this is the last time the jerk will do business with TTG."

The fire in her eyes told Jack that was a safe bet.

"Keep your fingers crossed the replacements get here before the real hordes descend," she muttered as she began pouring champagne into the tall crystal flutes.

He nodded toward the crowd emerging from the bank of elevators. "I think they're descending."

"Crap." She slapped the filled flutes onto a tray and hooked a finger at one of the waitstaff. "You're over twenty-one, right?"

"Right."

"Take this and start circulating."

"I'm a food server," he protested.

"Not for the next half hour, you're not. Take it! I've cleared it with your boss."

Champagne sloshing, she thrust the tray at him and reached under the counter for more flutes.

"Good thing the subcontractors aren't union," she said fervently. "My ass would be grass if I got TTG crosswise of the culinary workers and bartenders local."

Jack eyed the racks of glasses, bottles and nozzles behind the counter. Everything appeared to be clearly labeled.

"I've fixed a few martinis and Manhattans in my time. I'll pull bar duty until your replacements arrive. You go do your thing in the media center."

"No way! I can't let you sling booze. You're a guest."

"I won't tell if you don't. Go. I've got this."

Jack had no trouble interpreting the emotions that flashed across her expressive face. He could tell the instant the idea of John Harris Mason III dishing up drinks at Global Protective Service's big bash struck her as too irresistible to pass up.

"All right," she conceded, laughter sparkling in her eyes. "But let's hope Nicole doesn't hear about this. My ass won't just be grass. It'll be mowed and mulched."

"And it's such a nice ass." He couldn't help it. He had to reach behind her and caress the body part under discussion. "Trust me, sweetheart, I won't let anyone mow or mulch it."

She backed away and tried to look stern, but the light still danced in her eyes. "I can't believe you just did that."

Jack couldn't believe it, either. He'd do it again, though, in a heartbeat. Or better yet, drag her upstairs to that bridal suite she'd mentioned and caress a whole lot more than her ass. Sanity intruded in the form of the gray-haired senior senator from Virginia.

Thomas Dillon broke away from the group he was with and strolled over to the bar. "Jack?"

The senator looked from him to Gina and back again. Clearly he didn't understand what an ambassador-at-large was doing behind the drinks counter, but he contained his confusion behind a broad smile.

"I thought I recognized you, son. How's your father?"

"He's still kicking butt and taking names, Senator. What can I get you to drink?"

"Pardon me?"

"I'm pulling special duty tonight. What would you like?"

Despite the near-disastrous start, the remainder of the event went off without a hitch. Most of the invitees were jaded Washingtonians who had attended too many black-tie functions to do more than guzzle down the free booze and food, but Jack heard more than one guest comment on the quality of both.

His replacement arrived before he'd had to mix up more than a dozen drinks. He surrendered his post with some reluctance and mingled with the other guests. Jaded they might be, but the arrival of the movie's star started a low buzz. Gina had returned to the plaza and stood next to Jack while Dirk West graciously made the rounds.

"Wow," she murmured, eyeing his shaved head and six-feet-plus of tuxedo-covered muscle. "He looks tougher in real life than he does on the screen."

Tough, and extremely savvy. West worked the crowd like a pro and seemed to sense instinctively the real power brokers and potential backers. He might have been aided in that by the CEO of Global Protective Services, who stuck to the star's side like a barnacle and made a point of steering him over to Jack.

"This is Ambassador John Harris Mason," he said by way of introduction. "He's the man who faced down a cell of armed insurgents in Mali a few years ago."

"I read about that." West crunched Jack's hand in his. "Sounded like a pretty hairy situation. I might have to send a script writer to ferret out the details that didn't get into print."

Jack could have told him not to bother since most of the details were still classified but West had already turned his attention to Gina.

"And who's this?"

The bronze-edged name tag pinned to her lapel should have given him a clue. He ignored it, concentrating all his star power on her face.

"Gina St. Sebastian." She held out her hand and had it enfolded. "I'm with the Tremayne Group. We're coordinating this event."

West's appreciative gaze made a quick trip south, edged back up. "You ever considered taking a shot at acting, Ms. St. Sebastian?"

"I've toyed with the idea once or twice."

"If you decide to do more than toy, you give me a call."

Global's CEO was more interested in Jack's connections

at the State Department than the acting aspirations of the hired hands.

"I hear you've got a meeting with the Senate Intelligence Committee next week regarding embassy security, Ambassador. I've got some ideas in that regard."

"I'm sure you do."

"I'd like to discuss them with you. I'll have my people call and set up an appointment."

His mission accomplished, he steered West to the next group. Jack waited until they were out of earshot to fill Gina in on his conversation with his parents.

"I got ahold of my folks. They're anxious to meet you, but mother's chairing a charity auction tomorrow evening so I told them we'd drive down for Sunday brunch."

"Sunday brunch works for me."

"Good. That leaves tomorrow for just you and me."

She started to comment, but spotted the plump brunette with the radio clipped to her waist signaling from across the plaza.

"Gotta go. It's almost showtime."

She turned, spun back and flashed one of her megawatt smiles.

"Thanks for helping out earlier. Remind me to pay you for services rendered."

"I will," he murmured to her retreating back. "I most certainly will."

Jack carried fantasies of the various forms that payment might take with him into the plush media hall. They teased his thoughts all through Dirk West's explosive attempts to single-handedly save the world from evil. But not even his wildest imaginings could compete with reality when a tired but triumphant Gina invited him up to the bridal suite several hours later.

Eight

Gina had tried to convince Jack he didn't need to hang around while she signed off on the final tally sheets and supervised the breakdown. She'd honestly tried. Yet she couldn't suppress a little thrill of pleasure when he insisted on waiting for her to finish up.

So she'd extended the invitation to join her upstairs. When they entered the lushly appointed suite, though, all she wanted to do was plop down on the sofa, kick off her shoes and plunk her feet on the coffee table. Which was exactly what she did. And all she would have done if Jack hadn't plopped down beside her!

"That's some view," he commented lazily, his eyes on the dramatic vista of the floodlit capital dome framed by the suite's windows.

"Mmm."

She only half heard him. Her mind was still decompressing after the pressure-packed night. He responded by tugging loose his bow tie and popping the top button of his dress shirt before patting his lap.

"Here."

She blinked, suddenly very much in the present. She didn't trust either his simple gesture or her body's instant response to it. He read the sudden wariness in her face and patted his thighs again.

"I've been told I give a pretty good foot massage. Swing your feet up and see if you agree."

Oooooh, yeah! Gina most definitely agreed. Ten seconds after he went to work on her toes and arch, she was approaching nirvana. Groaning with pleasure, she wedged deeper into the corner of the sofa.

"If you ever decide to give up ambassadoring, you could make a bundle plying the foot trade."

"I'll keep that in mind."

Curious, she eyed him through the screen of her lashes. "What *are* you going to do when you give up ambassadoring?"

"Good question."

His clever, clever fingers worked magic on the balls of her right foot before moving to the left.

"What about those PACs I read about?" she asked. "The ones that think you've got the makings of a future president?"

"*Future* being the operative word. There are a few steps I'd have to take in between."

"Such as?"

"Running for public office, to start with. I've been just a career bureaucrat up to this point."

"Su-u-ure you have. I wonder how many career bureaucrats go toe-to-toe with armed terrorists."

"Too many, unfortunately. Still, elected office is almost a required stepping stone to anything higher. Except for the war heroes like Washington and Eisenhower, almost all of our presidents served as either governors or members of Congress."

"So run for governor. Or Congress. You'd make a great senator or representative. More to the point, someone's got to get in there and straighten out that mess."

"Am I hearing right?" Ginning, he pulled on her toes.

"This enthusiastic endorsement can't be coming from the same woman who's called me obnoxious and uptight and a few other adjectives I won't repeat."

"You are obnoxious and uptight at times. Other times..." She circled a hand in the air, trying to pluck out one or two of his less irritating traits. "Other times you surprise me, Mr. Ambassador. Like tonight, for instance, when you got behind the bar. You went above and beyond the call of duty there."

"I'm a man of many talents," he said smugly. "And that reminds me. I was promised payment for services rendered."

"So you were. Have you given any thought to what form that payment should take?"

"Oh, sweetheart, I haven't thought of anything else all evening."

Red flags went up instantly. Gina knew she was playing with fire. Knew the last thing she should do was slide her feet off his lap and curl them under her, rising to her knees in the process.

All she had to do was look at him. The tanned skin, the white squint lines at the corners of his eyes, the square chin and the strong, sure column of his throat. Like a vampire hit with a ravenous hunger, her weariness disappeared in a red flash. She had to taste him. Had to lean forward and press her mouth to the warm skin in the V of his shirt. Had to nip the tendons in his neck, the prickly underside of his chin, the corner of his mouth.

And of course, he had to turn his head and capture her lips with his. There was nothing gentle about the kiss. Nothing tentative. It went from zero to white-hot in less than a heartbeat. Mouths, teeth, tongues all engaged. Hips shifted. Hands fumbled. Muscles went tight.

Jack moved then, tipping her back onto the cushions. He came down with her, one leg between hers, one hand brushing her hair off her face. Careful not to put all his weight on her middle but taut and coiled and hungry.

She could feel him get hard against her hip. The sensation shot a hot, fierce rush through her veins. Shoving his jacket lapels aside, she tugged his starched shirt free of the satin cummerbund and tore at the buttons. When she got to the shoulder muscle underneath, she ran her palm over the smooth curve, then felt it bunch under her fingers as Jack's hand went to her waist. The two buttons on her borrowed sequin jacket proved a flimsy barrier. Jack peeled back the lapels and came to a dead stop. Every muscle and tendon in his body seemed to freeze.

"God."

It was half prayer, half groan. His brown eyes hot with desire, he brushed a finger along the lace trimming her demi-bra.

"Good thing I didn't know this was all you had on under those sequins. It was hard enough making it through the movie."

Gina tucked her chin and surveyed her chest with something less than enthusiasm. The underwired half cup of black silk and lace mounded her breasts almost obscenely.

"I've gone up another whole size," she muttered in disgust. "I had to buy all new bras."

Jack picked up on her tone and wisely didn't comment. Good thing, because she probably wouldn't have heard him. All it took was one brush of his thumb over her sensitized nipple and she was arching her back. And when he tugged down the lace and caught the aching tip between his teeth, every part of her screamed with instant, erotic delight.

She arched again, and he took what she offered. His hands and mouth and tongue drove her higher and higher. The knee he wedged between her thighs and pressed against her center almost sent her over the edge.

"Wait!" Gasping, she wiggled away from the tormenting knee. "Wait, Jack!"

He raised his head, a shudder rippling across his face. Disgust followed a moment later.

"Sorry. That was a little more than you probably expected to pay for my bartending services."

When he started to sit up, Gina grabbed his lapels and kept him in place. "Hold on, Ambassador. That little tussle doesn't even constitute minimum wage. I just…I just thought we should shed a few more layers."

Jack stared down at her, eyes narrowed. He knew as well as she did they wouldn't stop at a few layers. He was damned if he'd give her a chance to change her mind, though. Getting the stubborn Gina St. Sebastian into bed ranked almost as high up there as getting her to the altar.

"Shedding is good," he said with a crooked grin that masked his sudden iron determination. "I'll start."

His tux jacket hit the floor. The cummerbund and shirt followed a moment later. He held out a hand and helped her to her feet, taking intense satisfaction from the play of her greedy hands over his bare chest.

Once he'd disposed of the sequined jacket, he helped her shimmy out of her black satin pants. His self-control took a severe hit when he got a look at the hipsters that matched her black lace bra. They dipped to a low V on her still-flat belly and barely covered her bottom cheeks.

He cupped his hand over those sweet, tantalizing curves and brought her against him. He saw her eyes flare when she felt him against her hip, rock-hard and rampant. Her head tipped. Red singed her cheeks.

"Okay," she exhaled in a low, choked voice. "I really, really need to make payment in full. But the two of us going to bed together doesn't change anything."

The hell it didn't.

Jack kept that thought to himself as he scooped her into his arms and strode toward the bedroom.

The Tremayne Group had done their guest suite up right. A king-size bed sat on a raised dais, its chocolate-brown comforter draping almost to the floor. Mounds of brown, aqua and silver-trimmed pillows piled high against the padded headboard. Floor lamps gave the corners of the room a subdued glow, while a crystal dish filled with creamy wax pebbles emitted a faint scent of vanilla.

Jack absorbed the details with the situational awareness that was as much instinct as training. That alertness had kept him alive in Mali and served him well in so many other tense situations. But it shut down completely when he stretched Gina out on the soft, fluffy ocean of brown. Her hair spilled across the comforter in a river of pale gold. Her eyes were hot blue and heavy. Her long, lush body drove every thought from his mind but one.

Aching for her, he yanked down the zipper of his pleated black slacks. He discarded them along with his socks and jockey shorts, joined her on the bed and ran his hand over the flat planes of her belly.

"You are so incredibly gorgeous."

Her stomach hollowed under his palm even as she gave a breathless, delighted chuckle.

"Flattery will get you everywhere, Ambassador."

He slid his hand under the lace panties and found the wet heat at her center. Her head went back. Her lips parted. As Jack leaned down to cover her mouth with his, he realized he didn't want to be anywhere but here, with this woman, tasting her, touching her, loving her.

He was rougher than he'd intended when he stripped off her underwear. More urgent than he ever remembered being when he pried her knees apart and positioned himself between her thighs. And when she hooked her calves around his and canted her hips to fit his, he lost it.

Driven by a need that would shock the hell out of him when he analyzed it later, he thrust into her. It was a primal urge. An atavistic instinct to claim his mate. To brand her as his. Leave his scent on her. Plant his seed in her belly.

Except he'd already done that.

The thought fought its way through the red haze of Jack's

mind. He went stiff, his member buried in the hot satin that was Gina. Hell! What kind of an animal was he? He levered up on his elbows, blinking away the sexual mists that clouded his vision. When they cleared, he saw Gina glaring up at him.

"What?" she demanded.

"I didn't mean to be so rough. The baby…"

"Is fine! I, however, am not."

To emphasize her point, she hooked her calves higher on his and clenched her vaginal muscles. Jack got the message. Hard not to, since it damned near blew off the top of his head. He slammed his hips into hers again. And again. And again.

They could only spend so many hours in bed. Theoretically, anyway. Jack would have kept Gina there all day Saturday but even he had to come up for air. Since they wouldn't drive down to his parents' house in Richmond until the following day, he offered to show her his favorite spots in D.C. She approved the proposed agenda, with two quick amendments.

"I'd like to see where you live. And where you work."

Jack had no problem with either. Gina had packed clothes for the weekend but he had to get rid of his tux before he could appear in public again. That naturally lent itself to a first stop at his town house.

It was classic Georgetown. Three narrow stories, all brick. Black shutters. Solid brass door knocker in the shape of a horse's head. Gina's nose wrinkled when Jack mentioned that the detached garage at the back had once been slave quarters, but she was gracious enough to acknowledge he'd taken occupancy of the ivy-covered premises long after those tragic days.

The framed photo of Catherine still occupying a place of honor on the entryway table gave her pause, though. Almost as much as it gave Jack. He stood next to Gina as she gazed at the black-and-white photo.

It was one of his favorite shots. He'd taken it after losing yet another tennis match to his hypercompetitive wife. She laughed at the camera, her racquet resting on her shoulder. Her dark hair was caught back in a ponytail. A sweatband circled her forehead. All her energy, all her pulsing life, shone in her eyes.

"I bet she kept you jumping," Gina murmured.

"She did."

Almost too much.

The thought darted into Jack's mind before he could block it. That energy, that formidable legal mind, the all-consuming passion for politics. He'd had to march double time to keep up with her. More than once he'd wished she'd just relax and drift for a while.

The thought generated a sharp jab of guilt. Jack had to work to shrug it off as he left Gina to explore the town house's main floor and went upstairs to change. He came back down a half hour later, showered and shaved and feeling comfortable in jeans and his favorite University of Virginia crewneck.

"You sure you want to swing by my office? There's not a whole lot to see but we can make a quick visit if you want."

Gina forced a smile. The pictures of his wife scattered around the town house had gotten to her more than she would admit. She'd spotted several shots of Catherine alone. Several more of Catherine with Jack. The perfect marriage of smarts and ambition.

And here Gina was, trying desperately to anchor herself after years of flitting from job to job, man to man. Her life to this point seemed so frivolous, so self-centered. How could Jack have any respect for her?

She buried her crushing doubts behind a bright smile. "I've never been to the State Department. I'd like to see it."

"Okay, but don't say I didn't warn you."

Gina took Jack's disclaimer with a grain of salt. It should have been a teaspoon, she decided when he escorted her through State's echoing marble halls and into his impressive suite of offices.

The first thing she noticed was the view from the windows of the outer office. It cut straight down 21st Street to the Lincoln Memorial Reflecting Pool and presented a narrow, if spectacular, slice of Washington.

The second item that caught her attention was the individual in jeans, a button-down yellow shirt and round eyeglasses hunched over a computer. She shouldn't have been surprised that Jack's people were dedicated enough to come in on weekends. And when he introduced her to his chief of staff, she tried hard to bury her antipathy behind a friendly smile.

"I'm glad to finally meet you, Dale."

That was true enough. She'd been curious about this man. More than curious. She wasn't usually into stereotypes, but her first glimpse of Dale Vickers pegged him immediately as a very short, very insecure male suffering from a rampaging Napoleon complex. He kept his desk between him and his boss. Also between him and Gina. She had to reach across it to shake his hand. He acknowledged her greeting with a condescending nod and turned to his boss.

"I didn't know you were coming in this morning."

What a prick! Gina couldn't see why Jack put up with him until she spotted the framed 4x6 snapshot on the man's workstation. Catherine *and* Jack *and* Dale Vickers with their arms looped over each other's shoulders. All smiling. All wearing crimson sweatshirts emblazoned with the Harvard logo.

Images of Catherine Mason hovered at the back of Gina's mind for the rest of the day. She managed to suppress them while Jack gave her a private tour of the State Department's hallowed halls. Ditto when they took advantage of the glorious June afternoon to stroll the banks of the Potomac and cheer the scullers pushing against the vicious current.

After browsing the upscale shops in Georgetown Mall,

Jack took Gina to his favorite Thai restaurant later that evening. The owner greeted him with a delighted hand pump.

"Mr. Ambassador! Long time since we see you."

"Too long, Mr. Preecha."

The slender Asian whipped around, checked his tables and beamed. "You want by the window, yes? You and...?"

He made a heroic effort to conceal his curiosity when Jack introduced Gina. She felt it, though, and as soon as they were seated and their drink order taken, the question tumbled out.

"Did you and Catherine come here often?"

"Not often. We'd only lived in D.C. four or five months before she died. Do you like shumai? They serve them here with steamed rice and a peanut ginger sauce that'll make you swear you were in Bangkok."

The change of subject was too deliberate to ignore. Gina followed the lead.

"Since I have no idea what shumai are and have never been to Bangkok, I'll take your word on both."

Shumai turned out to be an assortment of steamed dumplings filled with diced pork, chicken or shrimp. She followed Jack's lead and dipped each morsel in ginger or soy sauce before gobbling it down. Between the dumplings, steamed rice, golden fried tofu triangles, some kind of root vegetable Gina couldn't begin to pronounce and endless cups of tea, she rolled out of the restaurant feeling like a python just fed its monthly meal. Too stuffed for any more wandering through Georgetown. Almost too stuffed for sex. When she tried to convince Jack of that sad state of affairs, though, he just laughed and promised to do all the work.

He followed through on his promise. The chocolate-brown sheets were a tangled mess and Gina was boneless with pleasure when he finally collapsed beside her.

For the second night in a row she fell asleep in his arms. And for the second morning in a row, she greeted the day cradled in the same warm cocoon.

She came awake slowly, breathing in Jack's scent, twitching her nose when his springy chest hair tickled her nose. It felt right to cuddle against his side. Safe and warm and right.

Slowly, without Gina willing them, the images she'd glimpsed of Jack's wife yesterday took form and shape in her mind. For an uneasy moment, she almost sensed Catherine's presence. Not hostile, not heartbroken at seeing her husband in bed with another woman, but not real happy, either.

"We'd better get up and get moving."

Jack's voice rumbled up from the chest wall her ear was pressed against. "Sunday brunch is a long-standing family tradition," he warned, stroking her hair with a lazy touch. "Hopefully, it'll just be us and my parents today but you should be prepared for the worst."

"Great! Now he tells me."

She could do this, Gina told herself as she showered and blow-dried her hair and did her makeup. She could run the gauntlet of Jack's family, all of whom had known and no doubt adored his wife. She wasn't looking forward to it, though.

And damned if she couldn't almost hear Catherine snickering in the steamy air of the bathroom.

Nine

Light Sunday–morning traffic was one of the few joys of driving in Washington. Jack's Range Rover whizzed through near deserted streets and crossed the 14th Street Bridge. The Jefferson Memorial rose in graceful symmetry on the D.C. side of the bridge. The gray granite bulk of the Pentagon dominated the Virginia side. From there they shot south on 395.

Once south of the Beltway, though, Jack exited the interstate and opted instead to drive a stretch of the old U.S. Highway 1. Gina understood why when he pulled into the parking lot of the Gas Pump Café just outside Woodbridge.

"We won't sit down for brunch until one or two. And this place," he said with a sweeping gesture toward the tin-roofed cafe, "serves the best biscuits and gravy this side of the Mason-Dixon line."

Gina hid her doubts as she eyed the ramshackle structure. It boasted a rusting, thirties-era gas pump out front. Equally rusty signs covered every square inch of the front of the building. The colorful barrage advertised everything from Nehi grape soda to Red Coon chewing tobacco to Gargoyle motor oil. The scents of sizzling bacon and smoked

sausage that emanated from the café, though, banished any
doubts the place would live up to Jack's hype.

It didn't occur to Gina that he'd made the stop for her sake
until they were seated at one of the wooden picnic tables. He
obviously didn't consider the slice of toast and half glass of
orange juice she'd downed while getting dressed adequate
sustenance for mother and child. She agreed but limited her
intake to one biscuit smothered in gravy, two eggs, a slab
of sugar-cured ham and another glass of juice. Since it was
just a little past nine when they rolled out of the café, Gina
felt confident she would be able to do justice to brunch at
one or two o'clock.

She also felt a lot more confident about meeting Jack's
family. Strapped into the Range Rover's bucket seat, she patted her tummy. "Hope you enjoyed that, baby. I sure did."

Jack followed the gesture and smiled. "Have you started
thinking about names?"

She didn't hesitate. "Charlotte, if it's a girl."

"What if it's a boy?"

She slanted him a sideways glance. He'd left his window
cracked to allow in the warm June morning. The breeze
lifted the ends of his dark gold hair and rippled the collar
of his pale blue Oxford shirt. He'd rolled the cuffs up on his
forearms and they, too, glinted with a sprinkling of gold.

She guessed what was behind his too-casual question. If
Jack won his on-going marriage campaign, he no doubt en-
visioned hanging a numeral after his son's name. John Harris
Mason IV. Not for the first time, Gina wondered if she was
being a total bitch for putting her needs before Jack's. Why
did she have to prove that she could stand on her own two
feet, anyway? This handsome, sophisticated, wealthy man
wanted to take care of her and the baby. Why not let him?

She sighed, acknowledging the answers almost before
she'd formulated the questions. She would hate herself for
giving up now. That had been her modus operandi her en-

tire adult life. Whenever she got bored or developed a taste for something new, she would indulge the whim.

But she couldn't quit being a mother. Nor did she want to give up a job she'd discovered she was good at. Really good. Then again, who said she had to quit? The Tremayne Group's Washington venue had plenty of business.

All of which was just a smoke screen. The sticking point—the real, honest-to-goodness sticking point—was that Jack didn't love her. He'd been completely honest about that. Although…the past two nights had made Gina begin to wonder if what they did feel for each other might be enough. Uneasy with that thought, she dodged the issue of boys' names.

"I haven't gotten that far," she said lightly. "Tell me about your parents. Where they met, how long they've been married, what they like to do."

Jack filled the rest of the trip with a light-handed sketch of a family steeped in tradition and dedicated to serving others. His mother had been as active in volunteerism over the years as his father had in his work for a series of presidents.

Gina might have been just the tiniest bit intimidated if she hadn't grown up on stories of the literary and social giants Grandmama had hobnobbed with in her heyday. Then, of course, there was her title. Lady Eugenia Amalia Thérèse St. Sebastian, granddaughter to the last Duchess of Karlenburgh. That and five bucks might get her a cup of coffee at Starbucks but it still seemed to impress some people. Hopefully, she wouldn't have to resort to such obvious measures to impress Jack's folks.

She didn't. Fifteen minutes after meeting John II, Gina knew no title would dent the man's rigid sense of propriety. He did not approve of her refusal to marry his only son and give his grandson the Mason name.

"Now, John," his wife admonished gently. She was a softspoken Southern belle with a core of tempered steel beneath her Donna Karan slacks and jewel-toned Versace tunic. "That's a matter for Gina and Jack to decide."

"I disagree."

"So noted," Ellen Mason said dryly. "Would you care for more iced tea, Gina?"

There were only the four of them, thank goodness. They were sitting in a glass-enclosed solarium with fans turning overhead. A glorious sweep of green lawn shaded by the monster oaks that gave the place its name filled the windows. The Masons' white-pillared, three-story home had once been the heart of a thriving tobacco plantation. The outlying acres had been sold off over the decades, but the current owner of Five Oaks had his lord-of-the-manner air down pat.

"I'd better not," Gina replied in response to Ellen's question. "I'm trying to cut out caffeine. Water with lemon would be great."

Jack's mother tipped ice water from a frosted carafe and used silver tongs to spear a lemon wedge. "We didn't worry about caffeine all those years ago when I was pregnant. That might explain some of my son's inexhaustible energy."

Her guest kept a straight face, but it took some doing. Ellen's son was inexhaustible, all right. Gina had the whisker burns on her thighs to prove it.

"I know you must have questions about this side of your baby's family tree," the older woman was saying with a smile in her warm brown eyes. "We have a portrait gallery in the upper hall. Shall I give you a tour while Jack and his father catch up on the latest political gossip?"

"I'd love that."

The duchess had taken Gina and Sarah to all the great museums, both at home and abroad. The Louvre. The Uffizi. The Hermitage. The National Gallery of Art in Washington. As a result Sarah had developed both an interest in and an appreciation for all forms of art. Gina's knowledge wasn't anywhere near as refined but she recognized the touch of a master when she saw it. None of the portraits hanging in the oak-paneled upstairs hall had that feel. Still, the collection offered a truly fascinating glimpse of costumes and hairstyles from the 17th century right down to the present.

Gina paused before the oil of Jack's grandfather. He wore the full dress uniform of an army colonel, complete with gold shoulder epaulets and saber. "My grandmother knew him," she told Ellen. "She said he and your mother-in-law attended a reception she once gave for some sultan or another."

"I've read about your grandmother," her hostess commented as they moved to the next portrait, this one of Ellen and her husband in elegant formal dress. "She sounds like an extraordinary woman."

"She is." Lips pursed, Gina surveyed the empty space at the end of the row. "No portrait of Jack and Catherine?"

"No, unfortunately. We could never get them to sit still long enough for a formal portrait. And…" She stopped, drew in a breath. "And of course, we all thought there was plenty of time."

She turned and held out both hands. Gina placed hers in the soft, firm fold.

"That's why I wanted this moment alone with you, dear. Life is so short, and so full of uncertainties. I admire you for doing what your heart tells you is right. Don't let Jack or his father or anyone else bully you into doing otherwise."

The brief interlude with Ellen made her husband a little easier to bear. John II didn't alter his attitude of stiff disapproval toward Gina but there was no disguising his deep affection for his son. He not only loved Jack. He was also inordinately proud of his son's accomplishments to date.

"Did he tell you he's the youngest man ever appointed as an ambassador-at-large?" he asked during a leisurely brunch that included twice-baked cheese grits, green beans almondine and the most delicious crab cakes Gina had ever sampled.

"No, he didn't," she replied, silently wishing she could

sop up the béchamel sauce from the crab cakes with the crust of her flaky croissant.

"Then he probably also didn't tell you some very powerful PACs have been suggesting he run for the U.S. Senate as a first step toward the White House."

"Dad…"

"Actually," Gina interrupted, "I read about that. I know those PACs love Jack. And he and I talked about his running for office the other night."

John II paused with his knife and fork poised above his food. "You did?"

"Yep. I told him he should go for it."

"Dad…"

Once again the father ignored the son's low warning. His lip curled, and a heavy sarcasm colored his voice. "I'm sure our conservative base will turn out by the thousands to support a candidate with an illegitimate child."

"That's enough!"

Jack shoved away from the table and tossed down his napkin. Anger radiated from him in waves. "We agreed not to discuss this, Dad. If you can't stick to the agreement, Gina and I will leave now."

"I'm sorry." The apology was stiff but it was an apology. "Sit down, son. Please, sit down."

Ellen interceded, as Gina suspected she had countless times in the past. "Jack, why don't you take our guest for a stroll in the rose garden while I clear the table and bring in dessert?"

Gina jumped up, eager for something to do. "Please, let me help."

"Thank you, dear."

A decadent praline cheesecake smoothed things over. Everyone got back to being polite and civilized, and Ellen deftly steered the conversation in less sensitive channels.

Gina thought they might make it through the rest of the

visit with no further fireworks. She nursed that futile hope right up until moments before she and Jack left to drive back to Washington. At his mother's request, he accompanied her into her study to pick up a flyer about an organization offering aid to abused children overseas she wanted him to look at.

That left Gina and John II standing side by side in the foyer for a few moments. An uncomfortable silence stretched between them, broken when he made an abrupt announcement.

"I had you investigated."

"What?"

"I hired a private investigator."

Gina's brows snapped together, and her chin tipped in a way that anyone familiar with the duchess would have recognized immediately as a warning signal.

"Did you?"

"I wanted him to chase down rumors about the other men you might have been involved with."

Her hand fluttered to her stomach in a protective gesture as old as time. "The other men I might have screwed, you mean."

He blinked at the blunt reply, but made no apology. "Yes."

The thought of a private investigator talking to her friends, asking questions, dropping insinuations, fired twin bolts of anger and mortification. Gina's chin came up another inch. Her eyes flashed dangerously.

"Why go to the expense of a private investigator? A simple DNA test would have been much cheaper."

"You were in that clinic in Switzerland. Jack flew over right after you called him. I told him to insist on a paternity test, but..." He broke off, grimacing. "Well, no need to go into all that now. What I want to say is I accept that you're carrying my grandchild."

"How very magnanimous of you."

The icy response took him aback. He looked as though

he wanted to say more, but the sound of footsteps stilled him. Both Jack and his mother sensed the tension instantly. Ellen sighed and shook her head. Her son demanded an explanation.

"What's wrong?"

"Nothing," Gina said before his father could respond. "Nothing at all. Thank you for a lovely lunch, Ellen."

She kissed the older woman's cheek before offering a cool glance and a lukewarm handshake to Jack's father.

"Perhaps I'll see you again."

He stiffened, correctly interpreting the threat buried in that polite "perhaps."

"I certainly hope so."

"All right," Jack said as the Range Rover cut through the tunnel of oaks shading the drive. "What was that all about?"

Gina wanted to be cool about it, wanted to take the high road and shrug off the investigation as inconsequential, but her roiling emotions got the better of her. She slewed around as much as the seat belt would allow. Anger, hurt and suspicion put a razor's edge in her words.

"Did you know your father hired a P.I. to investigate me?"

"Yes, I…"

"With or without your approval?"

"Christ, Gina." His glance sliced into her. "What do you think?"

She was still angry, still hurt, but somewhat mollified by his indignation. Slumping against the seat back, she crossed her arms. "Your father's a piece of work, Ambassador."

Which was true, but probably not the smartest comment to make. Jack could criticize his father. He wouldn't appreciate an outsider doing so, however, any more than Gina would tolerate someone making a snide comment about the duchess. The tight line to Jack's jaw underscored that point.

"I'm sorry," she muttered. "I shouldn't have said that."

He accepted the apology with a curt nod and offered one

of his own. "I'm sorry, too. I should have told you about the investigation. The truth is I didn't know about it until after we got back from Switzerland and then it just didn't matter."

Her anger dissipated, leaving only an urgent question. "Why not, Jack? Didn't you...? Don't you have any doubts?"

"No. Not one." The rigid set to his shoulders eased. His reply was quiet and carried the ring of absolute truth. "We may disagree on a number of important issues, marriage included, but we've always been honest with each other."

Her eyes start to burn. She refused to cry, she flatly refused, but she suddenly felt miserable and weary beyond words. "Look," she said tiredly, "this has been a busy few days. I may have overdone it a bit. I think...I think I'd better fly back to New York this evening."

He knifed her a quick look. "Is it the baby?"

"No! The baby's fine."

"Then it's my father." Another sharp glance. "Or is it us?"

"Mostly us." She forced a smile. "You have to admit we didn't get much sleep the past two nights. I need to go home and rack out."

"Is that what you really want?"

"It's what I really want."

The drive back to D.C. took considerably less time than the drive down to Richmond. No cutting off to ramble along Route 1. No stops at picturesque cafés. Jack stuck to the interstate, and Gina used the time to check airline schedules. She confirmed a seat on a 7:20 p.m. flight to New York. It was a tight fit, but she could make it if she threw her things in her weekender and went straight to the airport.

"You don't have to wait," she told Jack as he pulled into the parking garage at L'Enfant Plaza. "I can grab a cab."

"I'll drive you."

She was in and out of TTG's guest suite in less than twenty minutes. A quick call ensured the cleaning crew would come in the following day. The key cards she sealed in an envelope and slid under the door to the main office. Elaine Patterson, manager of the Washington venue, was due back tomorrow. Gina would coordinate the after-event report with her and tie up any other loose ends by email.

Her emotions were flip-flopping all over the place again when Jack pulled up at the airport terminal. Part of her insisted she was doing the right thing. That she needed to pull back, assess the damage to her heart done by the nights she'd spent in his arms. The rest of her ached for another night. Or two. Or three.

If Jack were experiencing the same disquiet, it didn't show. He left the Range Rover in idle and came around to lift out her weekender. His expression was calm, his hand steady as he buried it in her hair and tilted her face to his.

"Call me when you get home."

"I will."

"And get some rest."

"Yes, sir."

"I'll see you at our next doctor's appointment, if not before."

Before would be good, she thought as she closed her eyes for his kiss. Before would be very good.

When she climbed out of a cab outside the Dakota almost seven hours later, her ass was well and truly dragging. Her flight had been delayed due to mechanical problems before being canceled completely. The passengers had sat for well over an hour on the plane before being shuffled off and onto another. She'd called Jack once she was aboard the alternate aircraft so he wouldn't worry, and again when she landed at LaGuardia.

Since they'd touched down at almost midnight, she didn't call her grandmother. The duchess would have gone to bed hours ago and Gina didn't want to wake her. Feeling dopey with exhaustion, she took a cab into the city. Jerome wasn't on duty and she didn't know the new night doorman except to nod and say hello. Wheeling her suitcase to the elevator, she slumped against the mirrored wall as it whisked her upward.

The delicate scent of orange blossoms telegraphed a welcome to her weary mind. She dropped her purse and key next to the Waterford crystal bowl filled with potpourri. Her weekender's hard rubber wheels made barely a squeak as she rolled it over the marble tiles.

She'd crossed the sitting room and was almost to the hall leading to the bedrooms when she caught the sound of a muffled clink in the kitchen. She left the suitcase in the hall and retraced her steps. Light feathered around edges of the swinging door between the dining room and kitchen. Another clink sounded just beyond it.

"Grandmama?"

Gina put out a hand to push on the door and snatched it back as the oak panel swung toward her. The next second she was staring at broad expanse of black T-shirt. Her shocked glance flew up and registered a chin shadowed with bristles, a mouth set in a straight line and dark, dangerous eyes topped by slashing black brows.

Ten

Everything Gina had ever learned or heard or read about self-defense coalesced into a single, instinctive act. Whipping her purse off her shoulder, she swung it with everything she had in her.

"Hé!" The intruder flung up his arm and blocked the savage blow. *"Várj!"*

"Várj yourself, you bastard!"

Gina swung again. This time his arm whipped out and caught the purse strap. One swift tug yanked it out of her hands.

"If you've hurt my grandmother..."

She lunged past him into the kitchen. Her fingers wrapped around the hilt of the largest knife in the upright butcher-block stand.

"Jézus, Mária és József!" The stranger chopped his hand down on her wrist, pinning it to the counter. "Stop, Eugenia. Stop."

The terse command pierced her red haze of fear but her heart still slammed against her chest as the questions tumbled out. "How do you know my name? What are you doing here? Where's my grandmother?"

"The duchess is in her bedroom, asleep, I presume. I am

here because she invited my sister and me to stay. And I
know your name because we're cousins, you and I."

"Cousins?"

"Of a sort."

When she tugged her wrist, he released his brutal grip.
A smile softened the stark angles of his face. "I'm Dominic.
Dominic St. Sebastian. I live in Budapest, but my parents
came from Prádzec. Your grandmother's home," he added
when she looked at him blankly.

It took her a moment to recognize the name of the town
on the border between Austria and Hungary, in the heart of
what was once the Duchy of Karlenburgh.

"I don't understand. When did you get here?"

"This afternoon." He gestured behind him to the coffeemaker just starting to bubble and brew on the counter. "It's
midnight in New York, but morning in Hungary. My body
has yet to adjust to the time change and craves its usual dose
of caffeine. Will you join me for coffee and I'll explain how
Anastazia and I come to be here, in your home."

"No coffee," Gina murmured, her hand fluttering to her
stomach as she tried to absorb the presence of this dangerous-
looking man in her grandmother's kitchen.

He was as sleek and as dark as a panther. Black hair, black
shirt, black jeans slung low on his hips. The T-shirt stretched
taut across a whipcord-lean torso. The hair was thick and
razored to a ragged edge, as though he didn't have time or
couldn't be bothered with having it styled.

"Tea, then?" he asked.

"Tea would be good." Slowly getting her wind back, Gina
nodded to the cabinet behind his head. "The tea caddy is
in there."

"Yes, I know." His smile reached his eyes. "The duchess
told me to make myself to home. I took her at her word and
explored the cupboards."

Whoa! This man's face cast in hard angles and tight lines
was one thing. The same face relaxing into a lazy grin was

something else again. Gina had a feeling Dominic St. Sebastian could have his pick of any woman in Budapest. Or pretty much anywhere else in the world.

The fact that he knew his way around a tea caddy only added to the enigma. While the fresh-made coffee dripped into the carafe, he brewed a pot of soothing chamomile. Moments later he and Gina were sitting across from each other with steaming mugs in hand.

"So," he said, slanting her a curious look. "The duchess never spoke to you of me or my family?"

His speech held only a trace of an accent. A slight emphasis on different syllables that made it sound intriguing and sexy as all hell. Wondering where he'd learned to speak such excellent English, Gina shrugged.

"Grandmama told my sister and me that we had some cousins, four or five times removed."

"At least that many times. So we could marry if we wished to, yes?"

The tea sloshed in her mug. "Excuse me?"

"We're well outside the degree of kinship forbidden by either the church or the law. So we could marry, you and I."

A sudden suspicion darted into Gina's consciousness. Despite the duchess's seeming acceptance of her granddaughter's single-and-pregnant status, was she resorting to some Machiavellian scheming?

"Just when did my grandmother invite you and your sister to New York?"

"She didn't. I had to come on business and since Anastazia had never been to the States, she decided to accompany me. When we phoned the duchess to arrange a visit, she invited us for tea. She was so charmed by my sister that she insisted we stay here."

Charmed by his sister? Gina didn't think so.

"How long will you be in New York?"

"That depends on how swiftly I conclude my business. But not, I hope, before I get a chance to know you and the duchess. I've heard many tales of her desperate flight after the duke's execution."

"She doesn't speak of those days. I think the memories still haunt her."

"Is that why she's never returned to Austria, or traveled to any part of what is now Hungary?"

"I think so."

"That's certainly understandable, but perhaps some day she will visit and allow Anastazia and me to return her gracious hospitality. She would find everything much changed."

"I'm sure she would."

"You must come, too. I would enjoy showing you my country, Eugenia."

"Gina, please. Grandmama's the only one who calls me Eugenia, and then it's generally because I've screwed up."

"And does that happen often?"

She made a face. "Far more often than either of us would like."

The tea and the European rhythm of Dominic's speech had combined to bring Gina the rest of the way down from the adrenaline spike of her scare. When she reached bottom, weariness hit like a baseball bat.

Her jaw cracked on a monster yawn. She barely got a hand up in time to cover it and gave Dominic a laughing apology.

"Sorry 'bout that. It's been a long day."

"For me, also." His mesmerizing onyx eyes held hers. "Shall we go to bed?"

Okay, she had to stop attaching sexual innuendo to every word that came out of the man's mouth.

They took their mugs to the sink. Dominic rinsed them while Gina emptied the coffeemaker. He flicked off the kitchen light as they passed through the swinging door, plunging them both into temporary blindness.

Gina had grown up in this apartment and was intimately familiar with every piece of furniture a mischievous girl could crawl under or hide behind. She also knew which sharp edges to avoid, blind or not. Instinctively, she angled to the left to skirt the corner of a marble-topped table.

The move brought her into contact with Dominic's thigh, and his hand shot out to save her from what he must have assumed was a near fall.

"Careful."

For the second time that night he'd captured her arm. Gina wasn't quite as quick to shake off his hold this time.

"Thanks. I assume Grandmama put Anastazia in my sister's room and you in the study?"

"Is the study the baronial hall with the oak paneling and crown molding?" he asked dryly.

"It is." They stopped outside the double sliding doors. "Here you go. I guess I'll see you in the morning. Correction. Make that later in the morning."

His fingers slid from her forearm to her elbow to her wrist. Raising her hand, he bowed and dropped a kiss on it with old-world charm right out of the movies.

"*Aludj jól,* Gina."

"And that means?"

"Sleep well."

"*Aludj jól,* Dominic."

She left him standing by the sliding doors and reclaimed her suitcase. No light shone from under the door to her grandmother's room, so Gina slipped quietly into her own. She was asleep almost before her head hit the pillow.

She woke mere hours later. Grunting at what felt like a bowling ball resting atop her bladder, she rolled out of bed and headed for the bathroom.

When she snuggled between the sheets again, sleep didn't descend as swiftly. And when it did, it brought confusing dreams of a shadowy figure whose hair morphed from black to gold to black again.

Since Samuel wasn't expecting her back from Washington for another day, possibly two, Gina didn't feel compelled to go in to the office the next morning. Good thing, because she didn't wake up a second time until almost nine.

She took her time in the shower, wondering if she'd dreamed that kitchen encounter last night. It was so surreal, and so unlike her grandmother to invite complete strangers to stay in their home. Maybe she was more tied to the land of her birth than she let on.

Gina followed the scent of coffee and cinnamon toast to the kitchen, where Maria was turning fresh toast onto a plate.

"There you are. Dominic told us, *la duquesa* and me, that you came in late last night."

"I just about jumped out of my skin when I came in last night and bumped into him." Dying for a cup of coffee, Gina poured a glass of apple juice instead. "I'm surprised Grandmama invited him and his sister to stay here."

"Me, as well. But they are very nice and have made your grandmother smile. You will see," Maria said, flipping the last of the toast onto the platter.

"Here, I'll take that."

The scene in the sunny, green-and-white breakfast room certainly seemed to give credence to Maria's comment. The duchess was holding court, her snowy hair in a crown of braids, her chin feathered by the high lace collar of her favorite lavender silk blouse. Her smile was far from regal, though. Wide and lively, it transformed her face as she carried on an animated conversation with her guests in their native language.

But it was those guests who stopped Gina in her tracks. In the bright light of day, Dominic appeared every bit as dangerous as he had last night. Must be that European, unshaved whisker thing. Or his preference for black shirts. This one was starched cotton and open-collared, showing just a hint of a silver chain at his throat.

The woman seated across from him was almost as riveting. Her hair fell well past her shoulders, as lustrous and raven-black as her brother's. Her cheekbones were high and sharp, her mouth a glistening red. Thick lashes framed dark eyes with just the hint of a slant. If the rest of her was as striking as that sculpted face, the woman could walk into any modeling agency in New York and sign a high six-figure contract within minutes.

All of a sudden Gina felt fat and dumpy and just a tad jealous of the way these two outsiders seemed to have glommed on to her grandmother. That lasted only until the duchess spotted her. Her lined face lit up with love.

"You're awake at last. Come and join us, dearest."

Dominic pushed back his chair and took the platter of toast so Gina could bend to give her grandmother a kiss. The look he gave her banished any lingering nasty thoughts. Fat and dumpy wouldn't have put such an admiring gleam in his eyes.

"Good morning, cousin. Did you sleep well?"

"Very."

"You must let me introduce my sister. Anastazia, this is…"

"Eugenia Amalia Therése," the brunette said in an accent noticeably heavier than her brother's.

She, too, pushed back her chair and came around the table. Holding out both hands, she kissed Gina's cheeks. "I have been so eager to meet you, cousin. I, too, was named for the Archduchess Maria Amalia of Parma." She wrinkled her perfect nose. "I am Anastazia Amalia Julianna. Such long names we have, yes?"

Despite her cover-model looks, she was open and friendly and engaging. Gina couldn't help but smile back.

"We do indeed."

"You must call me Zia. And I will call you Gina."

That thorny matter settled, they joined the others at the table. Gina helped herself to two slices of cinnamon toast while her grandmother gave them all a rare glimpse into the family archives.

"Poor Archduchess Maria Amalia," she said with a wry

smile. "Married against her will to a mere duke while two of her sisters became queens. Marie Antoinette of France and Marie Caroline of Naples and Sicily."

Charlotte took a sip of her tea and shared another historical tidbit.

"The three sisters were reportedly very close. They often exchanged letters and portraits and gifts. One of the last letters Marie Antoinette smuggled out of her prison was to Amalia."

"I'm told there's a miniature of their mother, the Empress Marie Therese of Austria, in your Metropolitan Museum of Art," Zia said eagerly. "It is one of the places I hope to visit while I am here."

"You must get Eugenia to take you. She spent many hours at the Met as a child."

"Oh, but I must not impose." The brunette turned her brilliant smile on Gina. "From what your grandmother has told us, you're very busy with your work."

"Actually, I'm off today. We can go this afternoon, if you like."

"I would! And you, Dom. You must come, too, to see this long-dead ancestor of ours."

His gaze met and held Gina's. His mouth curled in a slow smile. "I'll have to see if I can reschedule my afternoon appointment."

Gina didn't get a chance to corner her grandmother until midmorning. Zia had gone out onto the terrace to check her phone for voice messages and emails. Dominic retreated to the study to make some calls. As soon as he was out of the room, Gina pounced.

"Okay, Grandmama, 'fess up. What's behind this sudden spurt of hospitality to distant relatives you've never met."

"Really, Eugenia! I should hope I'm not so lacking in generosity as to let two young and very charming relations stay in a hotel when we have plenty of room here."

"But you don't know anything about them."

"That's what Dominic said when I extended the invitation. He tried to refuse, but I insisted."

"Did either of them tell you what they do for a living?"

"Dominic does some kind of security work. Anastazia just got her MD degree from Semmelweis University in Budapest."

Gorgeous and smart and a doc. Another nasty little worm of jealousy poked its head up. Gina might have started feeling dumpy and fat again if Dominic hadn't come back into the room.

"I'm yours for the afternoon, if you're sure you wish to…"

He broke off and pivoted on the balls of his feet in the direction of the hall. Startled, Gina strained to hear in the sudden silence and picked up a faint buzz.

"Oh, that's my phone. I left it in my purse on the hall table last night. Excuse me."

The call had already gone to voice mail when she fished the phone out of her jam-packed bag. She saw the name on caller ID and stabbed the talk button just in time.

"Hello, Jack."

"Hi, Gina. I just wanted to check and see how you're feeling after your long odyssey last night."

The sound of his voice stirred the usual welter of confused emotions. Despite her abrupt departure yesterday, she couldn't believe how much she missed him. How much she ached for him.

"I'm good," she said, "although I decided not to go in to work since I had the day off, anyway."

"So you're going to put your feet up and rest, right?"

"Pretty much. Although I did agree to take my cousins to the Met this afternoon."

"Cousins?"

"Two of them. Dominic and his sister, Anastazia. Their parents came from Prádzec, which was once part of the Duchy of Karlenburgh."

"And is now in Hungary."

Trust an ambassador-at-large to know that. The phone to her ear, Gina wandered toward the end of the hall. Dom sat next to her grandmother's chair and appeared to be amusing her with some anecdote.

"Did the duchess know they were coming?" Jack asked.

"They surprised her. Me, too! I thought Dom was a burglar when I came chest-to-chest with him last night."

"They were there, in the apartment when you got home?"

"They're staying here."

That was met with a short silence.

"What did you say their names were again?"

"Dominic and Anastazia St. Sebastian. She's just finished med school and he does something in security. Grandmama didn't get the specifics."

She caught a flash of sunlight as the terrace doors opened and Zia rejoined the group.

"Oh, there's Anastazia. I'd better go, Jack."

"Gina…"

"Yes?"

"About this weekend—"

"It was just me," she interrupted quickly. She hadn't had time to sort through everything that had happened during their days together. And the nights! Dear God, the nights.

"Chalk it up to hormones run amok. I'll talk to you soon, okay?"

"Okay."

She blew out a breath and hit the end button, but some of the emotions Jack had stirred must have shown in her face when she walked into the sitting room. She couldn't hide them from the duchess. Her faded blue eyes locked onto to Gina's.

"Who was that, dearest?"

"Jack."

"Hmm."

The odd inflection in that murmur snared the interest of

both guests. They were too polite to ask, however, and the duchess left it to Gina to elaborate.

"Jack Mason. He's an ambassador-at-large with the U.S. State Department in Washington."

Dominic's expression of casual interest didn't change but just for a second she thought she saw something flicker in his dark eyes. Like the duchess, he must have sensed there was more to the call than she wanted to reveal.

Oh, hell. Might as well let it all hang out.

"He's the father of my baby."

After Gina disconnected, Jack spent several long moments staring at the slice of the Mall viewable through his office windows. Their brief conversation ricocheted around in his mind.

Two of them. From Hungary. They surprised her. Chest-to-chest.

He wanted to believe it was his recent showdown with the Russian Mafia thugs who'd spilled across the borders of Eastern and Central Europe that prompted him to reach for the phone. Yet he couldn't get that chest business out of his head.

His chief of staff answered the intercom. "What's up, boss?"

"I need you to run a check on a pair from Hungary. They say they're siblings and are going by the names Dominic and Anastazia St. Sebastian."

Eleven

The next few days flew by. Gina got caught up at work. During her spare hours she showed Zia and Dominic the best of New York. She also delighted in the slow unfurling of her grandmother's memories. Prompted by her guests' presence and their gentle probing, the duchess shared some of her past.

She'd kept it locked inside her for so long that each anecdote was a revelation. Even now she would only share those memories that gave glimpses of a girl born into a wealthy, aristocratic family, one who'd grown up with all Europe as her playground. A fascinated Gina learned for the first time that her grandmother might have qualified as an Olympic equestrian at the age of fifteen had her family allowed her to compete. She'd retaliated for their adamant refusal by insisting she be allowed to study Greek and Roman history at Charles University in Prague.

"Prague is such a romantic city," the duchess mused to her audience of three over a dinner of Hungarian dishes prepared by Zia and Dominic as a small thank-you to their hostess.

Candles flickered in tall silver holders. The remains of the meal had been cleared away but no one was in a hurry to leave the table. A Bohemian crystal decanter of *pálinka* sat within easy reach. Double-distilled and explosively potent, the apricot-flavored brandy had been a gift from Zia and Dom. The duchess and her guests sipped sparingly from balloon-shaped snifters. Gina was more than content with a goblet of diet cranberry juice and the dreamy expression on her grandmother's face.

"That's where I first met the duke," the duchess related with smile. "In Prague. There'd been talk off and on about a possible liaison between our families but nothing had come of it at that point."

"So what was he doing in Prague?" Gina asked.

"He'd evidently decided it was time to take a wife, and came to find out if I was scandalously modern as the rumors said."

She took a sip of brandy and a faraway look came into her eyes.

"When he walked into the café where my friends and I were having dinner, I didn't know who he was at first. All I saw was this tall, impossibly handsome man with jet-black hair and the swarthy skin of his Magyar ancestors. Even then, he had such a presence. Every head in the café turned when he walked over to my table," she murmured. "Then he bowed, introduced himself, and I was lost."

The duchess paused, drifting on her memories, and Gina's gaze drifted to Dominic. His olive-toned skin and dark eyes indicted Magyar blood ran in his veins, too.

A nomadic, cattle-herding tribe that swept into Europe from the Steppes, the Magyars were often depicted in art and literature as the early Hungarian equivalent of America's Wild West cowboys. Gina was back in the 8th or 9th century, picturing Dominic riding fast and low in the saddle, when the intercom sounded.

She returned to the present with a start. The buzz brought the duchess out of her reverie, as well. A small frown of annoyance creased her forehead.

"I'll get it," Gina said.

She crossed to the intercom's wall unit and saw the flashing light signaling a call from the lobby. "Yes?"

"It's Jerome, Lady Eugenia. There's a gentleman to see you. Mr. John Mason."

Jack! Surprise and pure, undiluted delight flooded her veins.

"Send him up! Excuse me," she said to the three interested parties at the table. "I need to get the door."

She rushed to the entryway and out into the hall, wishing she'd spiffed up a little more for this evening at home. Oh, well, at least she still fit into her skinny jeans. And her crab-apple-green stretchy T-shirt did accent her almost-nursing-mother boobs.

When Jack stepped out of the elevator, Gina forgot all about her appearance and devoured his. Ohmanohman-ohman! Hungarian cowboys had nothing on tall, tanned Virginians.

The sight of him erased last weekend's awkward moments. Her hurt and indignation over learning that his father had hired a P.I. evaporated. Ditto the poisonous little barbs planted by his obnoxious chief of staff. Double ditto the ache in her heart when she'd spotted the pictures of Catherine at his home. Like the duchess had so many years ago, all Gina needed to do was look at this man and know she was lost.

"What are you doing here?"

"Two reasons. One, I didn't like the way our weekend ended. I'm still kicking myself for letting you leave with little more than a peck on the cheek."

"Oh. Well. I suppose we can correct that."

"You suppose right."

When he hooked her waist, she went into his arms eagerly, joyfully. He buried a hand in her hair and more than made up for any deficiencies in their parting.

Gina could have stayed there forever. The feel and the taste and the scent of him wrapped around her like warm silk. She felt his heart beating under her spread palms, breathed in the heady mix of aftershave and male.

When he raised his head, her heart was in her smile. "You said there were two reasons. What's the second?"

The pause was brief, hardly more than half a breath, but still noticeable.

"I missed you."

"Was it that hard to say?" she teased.

"You try it."

"I missed you." It came so easily she added a little embellishment. "Bunches."

The murmur of voices inside the apartment snagged Jack's attention. "Did I catch you at a bad time?"

"No, we finished dinner a while ago and are just sitting around the table talking. Come meet my cousins."

She led him to the dining room and had time to note widely varied reactions before she made the introductions. Zia's first glimpse of the newcomer brought her elbows off the table and a look of instant interest to her face. As her eyes raked Jack over, a slow, feline smile curved her lips.

Gina couldn't help herself. She was bristling like a barnyard cat when she noticed Dominic's expression. It was as shuttered as his sister's was open. The duchess's, on the other hand, was warm and welcoming.

"Good evening, Ambassador. It's good to see you again."

The title sent Zia's brows soaring. Her gaze whipped from Jack to Gina and back again, while Dominic slowly pushed his chair back from the table and stood.

"It's good to see you, too, Duchess." Jack crossed the dining room to take her hand. "I'm sorry to barge in like this."

"No need to apologize. Allow me to introduce my guests. They're visiting from Hungary."

"So Gina told me."

"Anastazia, may I present Ambassador Jack Mason."

He was at his most urbane with the sultry brunette. A smile, a lift of her hand, a light kiss on the fingers.

"You must call me Zia," she purred. "And I will call you Jack, yes?"

"Igen."

"How wonderful! You speak our language."

"Only enough to order a drink in a bar."

"In Hungary," she laughed, "that is more than enough. This is my brother, Dominic."

Jack rounded the table and extended his hand. It was a simple courtesy, a universal gesture recognized the world over. Yet there was something about the look accompanying it that made Gina pause. The message was subtle. Almost *too* subtle. She caught a hint of it, though, or thought she did.

So did Dominic. His smile took on a sardonic edge, his eyes a sudden glint as he shook Jack's hand.

"We've met before, Ambassador, although I doubt you'll remember."

"I remember. I also remember you were using another name at the time."

The two men ignored the surprise that produced among the women. Their gazes locked, they seemed to be engaged in a private and very personal duel.

"I was, indeed," Dominic drawled. "And you, as I recall, had not yet acquired your so very impressive diplomatic credentials."

The duchess's notions of propriety didn't include what was fast assuming the air of an Old West showdown in her dining room. With a touch of irritation, she thumped her hand on the table to get the combatant's attention.

"Do sit down, both of you. Jack, would you care to try this very excellent cognac? Or there's coffee if you prefer."

"Cognac, please."

"Gina, if you'll get another snifter perhaps Jack or Dominic will condescend to tell us where or when they met before."

The acidic comment found its mark. While Gina retrieved a cut crystal snifter from the graceful Louis XV china cabinet that took up almost an entire wall, the tension between the two men eased by imperceptible degrees. She brought the snifter to the table and splashed in the aromatic brandy as Dom yielded the floor to Jack with upturned palms.

"It's more your story than mine, Ambassador."

Jack accepted the snifter with a murmured thanks and addressed himself to the duchess. "Dominic and I met a number of years ago in Malta. I was on a UN fact-finding mission investigating the transshipment of young women kidnapped from Eastern Europe and sold to wealthy purchasers in the Arab world."

"Dear Lord!" The duchess shot her guest a sharp, questioning look, but he merely gestured for Jack to continue.

"While the UN team was in Malta, we heard rumors of a shipment coming in from Albania. We worked with Interpol and the Maltese authorities to intercept the trawler transporting the merchandise. There were six girls aboard, all between the ages of fifteen and twenty, all drugged to the gills."

Jack lifted the balloon goblet and swirled its contents. His gaze shifted from the duchess to the man sitting across of him.

"The captain of the trawler was killed in the cross fire. That's the word that was put out, anyway."

"What do you mean?" Gina demanded. "Was the captain killed or wasn't he?"

She didn't like where this was going. Had she and her grandmother been too trusting? Had they accepted too readily that Dom and Zia were who they said they were? With a sinking sensation, she remembered how dangerous Dom had seemed that first night, when she'd come home and surprised him in the kitchen.

"The captain went down," Jack confirmed, "but not in a cross fire. Evidently he spotted the intercept boats on his radar and started dragging the girls to the rail. He was going to throw them overboard and get rid of the incriminating evidence before we closed in. That's when he took a shot point-blank to the forehead."

Dom lifted a shoulder. "The bastard had one of those kids shoved against the rail. There was no time to negotiate."

"I don't understand." Gina frowned at her cousin. "Were you on one of the intercept boats?"

"I was on the trawler."

"What?"

He leaned forward, acknowledging her shock. "I was undercover, Gina. I'd been working to take down the head of that particular white slavery ring for months, but I couldn't allow the captain to murder those girls."

"Or blow your cover," Jack murmured in the stunned silence that followed.

Dom's glance slewed back to him. "Or blow my cover."

"Funny thing about that." Jack swirled his cognac again, his eyes never leaving Dom's face. "Interpol put out the word that the second crewman on the trawler escaped after being taken into custody. Yet there was never any record made of the arrest. And the officer who supposedly took the man into custody disappeared two days later."

Dom's smile didn't quite make it to his eyes. "The Albanians play rough."

Gina couldn't believe they were sitting in this elegant dining room, sipping brandy and cranberry juice from Baccarat crystal while calmly discussing kidnapped fifteen-year-olds and death on the high seas. She glanced at her grandmother and found the same incredulity on the duchess's face. Even Zia looked stunned. Evidently her brother's undercover persona was news to her, too.

"I'm curious," Jack said. "Where did you go from Malta, St. Sebastian?"

"I had several assignments. As did you, Mason."

"You're no longer with Interpol."

It was a statement, not a question, but Dominic responded

with a quick, slashing grin. "Not anymore. I'm now what you might term an independent entrepreneur."

And just like that, the ominous spell was broken. He was Gina's cousin again. Handsome, charming, exotic and more intriguing than she'd ever imagined.

She made the fatal mistake of saying so when she walked Jack to the door an hour later.

"I had no idea my cousin was an undercover agent."

"Isn't that the whole point of 'undercover'?"

The acerbic comment raised Gina's brows.

"I suppose," she replied. "But still, you have to admit it's all pretty James Bondish."

"If you say so. Are you tired?"

The abrupt change of subject made her blink. It also made her realize she wasn't the least tired. Probably because the hour was still relatively early. Either that, or the extraordinary conversation at the dinner table had stimulated her. Or just standing here, so close to Jack, set every one of her nerves to dancing.

"Not really. Why?"

"I'm staying at the Excelsior. It's only a few blocks from here. Do you feel like getting out for a little while? We still need to talk about last weekend."

Cold, hard logic dictated a negative. She still hadn't completely sorted through the confused feelings left over from their weekend together. Luckily, Gina had never been particularly concerned with logic. At that moment, looking up into Jack's brown eyes, all she knew was that she craved an hour or two or six alone with him.

She'd never been the kind to play games, much less hide her feelings. Coyness didn't factor anywhere into her makeup. A smile of eager anticipation slid into her eyes as she tipped her head toward the dining room.

"Hang loose. I'll tell Grandmama and the others not to wait up for me."

* * *

They opted to walk to the Excelsior. The June night was too balmy and the city lights too enticing to take a cab for a few short blocks. When they reached the lobby of the Dakota, she steered him away from the main entrance on West 72nd toward the inner courtyard.

"This way. It's shorter."

They exited on 73rd and cut back to Central Park West. Somehow Gina's hand found her way into Jack's as they strolled past the imposing bulk of the Museum of Natural History. And somehow, when they were in the elevator shooting up to his suite, his lips found hers.

She couldn't blame the heat that raced through her on hormones. It was Jack. All Jack. Only Jack. He stoked her senses. Fired her blood. She made herself wait until he keyed the door to his room before she pounced. Then there were no holds barred.

"I hope this is what you had in mind when you asked if I wanted to get out for a while," she muttered as she tore feverishly at his shirt buttons.

"Pretty much."

His voice was low and rough. So were his hands. Dragging up the hem of Gina's T-shirt, he cupped her aching breasts. All it took was one flick of his thumbs over her supersensitive nipples to have her moaning. On fire for him, she locked her mouth and her body with his. They were both half-naked when she threw a glance around the luxurious sitting room.

"There's a bed here somewhere, right?"

"Oh, yeah."

The bedroom was as palatial as the rest of the suite. All crown molding and watered silk wallpaper. Not that either of them noticed. The bed was the center of their focus. Four ornately carved posts. Champagne-colored gauze dripping from each corner. A silk duvet in the same color just begging to be yanked back.

Jack did the honors before tumbling Gina onto the cool sateen sheets. Standing beside the bed, he stripped off the rest of his clothes. Her greedy eyes feasted on his muscled chest. His washboard ribs and flat stomach. His rampant sex.

Gina had to cup him. Had to taste him. Rolling onto her knees, she scooted to the edge of the mattress and wrapped her hand around him. He was hot to her touch. Hot and ridged and already oozing. The milky bead at the tip of his erection stirred a deep, feminine thrill. The idea that she could bring her man to this point with just a kiss, just a stroke, set a torch to her own wild desire. Dipping her head, Gina took him in her mouth.

Jack stood it as long as he could. Then the atavistic need that had been building in him since the moment he'd walked into the duchess's apartment swept everything else aside. He wanted to claim this woman. Mark her as his.

Driven by that primal instinct, he pushed her onto the pillows and followed her down. She spread her legs for him willingly, eagerly, and Jack sank into her. Her hips rose, rammed into his. Once. Twice. Again. Then she opened her eyes and the red mist that had obscured Jack's mind cleared.

This was Gina of the bright, contagious smile.

Gina, who enticed and excited him.

Gina, who'd erased everything and everyone else from his mind.

Jack came out of a deep sleep with his customary, instant awareness. The hotel room was still dark, the silence deep, although a faint gray light was just beginning to show at the edge of the drapes blanketing the window.

Gina lay sprawled at his side. Soft puffs of air escaped her lips with each breath. Not quite snores but close enough to make him smile. With slow, careful moves he nudged down the knee digging into his hip and eased out of bed.

His slacks and shorts lay where he'd dropped them. He

pulled them on but left his belt unbuckled and shirt lying where it was as he crossed to the window. Lifting the drape a crack, he saw the city hadn't yet roared to life. Like Jack, it was enjoying the final quiet moments before the rush of the day.

He stared at the shadowy bulk of the Museum of Natural History across the street and tried to remember the last time he'd felt so relaxed. More important, the last time his world had felt so right. Not since Catherine, certainly.

Or even before.

The traitorous thought slipped in before he could block it. Only here, in the dim stillness, with Gina just a few feet away, could he admit the painful truth.

Catherine had been all brilliant energy. Athletic, competitive, totally committed to the causes she believed in. Loving and living with her had demanded the same high level output from Jack.

Would he have burned out? Would they?

Or would they have found what he'd somehow found so swiftly and so unexpectedly with Gina? Jack struggled to find the right word for it. It wasn't peace. Or contentment. Or certainty. God knew, there was nothing certain or predictable about Eugenia Amalia Therése St. Sebastian!

Nor was what he felt for her wrapped up in the baby. The fact she was carrying his child played, of course. No way it couldn't. But what had Jack by the throat right now was Gina. Just Gina.

Christ! Why didn't he just admit it? He was in love with her. Everything about her. Okay, she pissed him off royally at times. And yes, she was one of the most stubbornly hardheaded females he'd ever encountered. Yet everything inside him warmed at the thought of waking up next to her for the next…the next…

His jaw locked. Whirling, he strode back to the bed and sat on the edge.

"Gina. Wake up."

She grunted and tried to burrow into her pillow.

"Wake up."

"Wha…?" She raised a face half-obscured by a tangle of hair and blinked owlishly. "What?"

"Sit up a moment."

Grumbling, she rolled onto a hip and wiggled up against the headboard. The sheet came with her in a waterfall of Egyptian cotton.

"This better be good," she muttered.

She shoved her hair out of her face and tucked the sheet around her breasts, scowling at him through still sleepy eyes. He figured that was as good as he would get.

"Okay, here's the deal. I love you. I want to wake up beside you every morning for as long as we have together. The problem is, neither of us knows how long that might be."

He gripped her upper arms. His fingers dug into soft flesh as he pressed his point.

"I learned the hard way there are no guarantees. You… we have to grab whatever chance at happiness we have now, today. I understand you're still trying to sort through all the changes going on in your life right, but…"

"Wait! Just hold on!"

She pulled away from him, and Jack smothered a curse. He'd overplayed it. Pushed her too hard. He was falling back to regroup when she scrambled off the bed, sheet and all, and pointed a finger at him.

"You stay right where you are. I have to pee. And wash my face. And brush my teeth. Afterward, I'm going to come back to bed and you're going to repeat part of your speech."

"Which part?"

She looked over her shoulder on her way to the bathroom. The smile she sent him lit up the entire room.

"The I-love-you part."

Jack sat there, grinning like an idiot.

* * *

He was still grinning when he heard a faint click coming from the sitting room. A second later, the outer door thudded back against the wall and three men rushed in.

Jack reacted instantly. His one thought, his only thought, was to direct them away from Gina. Springing to the far side of the bed, he grabbed the only available weapon. He had his arm back to hurl the nightstand lamp when the bald giant leading the pack leveled a silenced semiautomatic. The beam of his laser sight painted a red eye dead-center in Jack's naked chest.

"Don't be foolish, Ambassador."

He recognized the voice even before Dominic St. Sebastian stepped from behind baldy's hulking frame.

Twelve

"Now," Gina said gleefully as she yanked open the bathroom door, "let's pick up where we…"

She stopped dead. Clutching the towel she'd wrapped around her like a sarong, she gaped in stunned disbelief at the frozen tableau that greeted her. Jack, gripping a table lamp like a baseball bat. A monster with a shaved head aiming a gun at his chest. Another stranger eying her half-naked body with a leer. And Dom, his dark eyes flashing an urgent message she couldn't even begin to interpret.

"Wh…?" She backed up an involuntary step, two, hit the bathroom door frame. "What…?"

"Very nice, Ambassador." The leering stranger's accent was so thick Gina's shocked mind could barely understand him. "Your woman would bring a good price, yes?"

"Jack! Dom!" Her frantic gaze whipped from one to the other. "What's going on?"

Dom stepped toward her, still telegraphing a signal that refused to penetrate her frantic brain.

"Listen to me, Gina. These men and I have some unfinished business to take care of, business that involves Jack. When you wake, you will understand."

"When I…when I wake?"

A small, apologetic smile altered his grim expression for a moment. Just long enough to distract Gina from the blow that clipped her chin and snapped her head back. She felt Dom catch her as she crumpled. Heard Jack snarl out a curse. Sensed some sort of violent movement on the other side of the room, followed by a low pop.

Then everything faded to black.

She came to slowly, dazed and disoriented. As the gray mist cleared, she discovered she was stretched on the unmade bed. Alone. With the towel draped over her naked body.

She also discovered that her jaw hurt like nobody's business. The ache cut through her lingering haze. A montage of images leaped into her head, sharp and cold and terrifying. The men. Dom. The gun with its ugly silencer.

"Jack!"

Terror engulfing her, Gina shoved off the bed. The violent lunge brought a dark, dizzying wave. She had to reach out a hand to steady herself for a moment, as the towel puddled around her ankles. As soon as the wave receded enough to reclaim her scant body covering, she rushed into the sitting room.

Nothing. No one. Not a table out of place. No overturned chairs. No Jack, or any strangers.

Or Dom.

She hadn't fully processed those moments right before her cousin clipped her, hadn't really understood the vivid images that had popped into her head. She strung them together now, and the pattern they formed made her want to retch.

Dom! Dear God, Dom! What was he involved in? Why had he led those men to Jack? What did they want?

Five exhausting hours later, Gina still didn't have an answer to any of those questions. Neither did the small army of city, state and federal officials who'd descended on the Excelsior in response to her 911 call.

Two uniformed NYPD officers arrived hard on the heels of hotel security. They were followed in a bewildering succession by two plainclothes detectives; a CSI team to scour the suite for fingerprints and other evidence; a grim-faced individual who identified himself as being with the city's counterterrorism unit; two agents from the regional FBI office; a liaison from the governor's office in Albany; a Department of Homeland Security rep and a tall, angular woman from the State Department's New York Office of Foreign Missions, who'd been sent at the urgent request of her boss to find out what the hell happened to Ambassador-At-Large Mason.

Senior FBI Agent Pamela Driskell assumed charge of the hastily assembled task force. It was done with tact and a smooth finesse that told Gina the agent had considerable prior experience dealing with prickly jurisdictional issues.

"Section 1114 of Title 18 U.S. Code assigns the FBI the responsibility for protecting officers and employees of the United States," she explained in a peaches-and-cream Southern drawl at odds with her short, no-nonsense hair and stocky frame. "Now tell me everything you know about this cousin of yours."

Gina started with the surprise visit by Dom and his sister and ended with last night's startling revelations.

"I didn't get all the details. Just that he and Jack—Ambassador Mason—crossed paths some years ago during a UN mission investigating white slavery."

Driskell shot a look at the State Department rep. "You know anything about that?"

"No, but I'll check it out."

Whipping out her BlackBerry, the woman turned away. Driskell swung back to Gina.

"What else?"

"Dom—my cousin—was an undercover agent at the time. Working for Interpol."

"That right? Well, we'll check that out, too. Now I think it's time we talk to your cousin's sister."

She flapped a hand to get the attention of everyone else in the suite.

"Y'all have any further questions for Ms. St. Sebastian? No? Okay, I'm taking her home. Kowalski and I will interview Anastazia St. Sebastian."

When Gina and her escort arrived, Jerome was at his station. Concern etched deep grooves in his seamed face, and his shocked gaze went to the bruise that had blossomed on her chin.

"It's not as bad as it looks," she assured the doorman.

Actually, it was worse but Jerome didn't need to know that.

"Two police officers arrived earlier," he reported.

Gina nodded. Driskell had requested NYPD dispatch the officers. Just in case Dom made an appearance.

"One officer's waiting in the lobby," Jerome said with a worried frown. "The other went up to the duchess's apartment. Can you tell me what's going on, Lady Eugenia?"

Special Agent Driskell started to intervene but Gina held up a palm. "It's okay. I've known this man all my life. I feel safer with him on the door than any five FBI agents."

Driskell hiked a brow but didn't argue the point. "We're investigating the suspected kidnapping of Ambassador Jack Mason," she said instead. "We have reason to believe Dominic St. Sebastian may be involved."

"No!" Jerome reeled back a step. "I don't believe it!"

"Why not?"

He had to stop and think about his instinctive denial. "I've seen Mr. St. Sebastian and his sister with the duchess," he said after a moment. "They're so good with her. So caring and solicitous."

Driskell's curled lip said what she thought of caring and solicitous. "What time did you come on duty this morning?"

"Nine o'clock."

Too late for the events that happened at the Excelsior hours earlier, but Driskell tried, anyway.

"Have you seen two men loitering anywhere in the vicinity? One big and bald? The other smaller, with a heavy accent?"

Jerome drew himself up, all wounded dignity under his summer uniform. "If I'd seen anyone loitering in the vicinity of the Dakota, you may rest assured I would have seen they were attended to."

"I'll take that as a no," Driskell said in her deceptively soft, magnolia-petal drawl.

The uniformed cop in the lobby reported no sighting of Dominic St. Sebastian, his suspected accomplices, or Ambassador Mason. The cop who'd been assigned to wait in the duchess's apartment gave the same report.

Gina only half heard him. Her attention went straight to her grandmother. The duchess sat as straight-spined as ever in her high-backed chair. Maria huddled with shoulders hunched in the chair beside hers. Both women showed worried, strained faces. And both jerked their heads up when Gina walked in.

"Eugenia!"

Relief flooded the duchess's face. Then she seemed to fold into herself, like someone who'd been granted a reprieve from her worst fears.

Gina rushed across the room and dropped to her knees beside the woman who'd always been her anchor. The terror she'd been holding at bay rose up again but she choked it back. She wasn't about to aggravate her grandmother's heart condition by indulging in a fit of hysterics like she really, really wanted to.

"I'm okay, Grandmama."

"What happened to your face?"

She hesitated but couldn't find any way around the truth. "Dom knocked me unconscious."

"No!"

The single syllable arced through the air like summer lightning. Sudden. Tense. Electrifying. Gina jerked her head around and saw Zia leap off the sofa. Her face was ablaze, her eyes feral.

"My brother would not strike a woman!"

"Guess again," Gina snapped.

"I don't believe you!"

The savage denial pulled her up short. Jerome and Anastazia. That made two people in less than five minutes who refused to accept Dom's role in the morning's events.

Her grandmother made a third.

"I can't believe it, either," the duchess said in a more shaky voice than Gina had ever heard coming from her. "Please, Eugenia. Introduce me to these people. Then for heaven's sake sit down and tell us what happened. Zia and Maria and I have been imagining every sort of horrible disaster."

The introductions didn't take much time. The telling took only a little longer. What could Gina add to the stark facts? She'd emerged from the bathroom. Found Dom and two strange men in Jack's suite. Dom stepped forward, knocked her out. She woke alone.

"I cannot understand any of this," Zia said fiercely. "But whatever happened, Dom had some reason for his actions."

Agent Driskell chose to exert her authority at that point. "We'd like to talk to you about your brother, Ms. St. Sebastian."

"It's Dr. St. Sebastian," Zia interrupted acidly.

"Right." The agent turned to the duchess. "Is there some place my partner and I can speak privately with Dr. St. Sebastian?"

"Yes, of course. Maria, will you show them to the breakfast room?"

The kitchen door swished behind them, leaving Gina and her grandmother alone for a few precious moments.

"Eugenia, for God's sake, be honest with me." The duchess held out a trembling hand. "Did you fall? Hurt yourself or the baby?"

"No." She took her grandmother's hand and sank into the chair Maria had just vacated. "Dom caught me before I hit the floor."

"He knocked you unconscious but didn't let you fall? This…none of this makes any sense."

"I know."

She was no closer to understanding when Agent Driskell and her partner departed some time later. Before leaving, Driskell gave Gina a business card imprinted with her office and cell phone numbers.

"There's a chance your cousin or whoever's he's working with may try to reach you. If they do, call me at once."

"I will," Gina promised, slipping the card into the pocket of her jeans. "And you'll call me immediately if they contact someone in Jack's office?"

Driskell nodded. "In the meantime, we'll pull the police officer here in the apartment but keep one in the lobby just in case."

With the agents' departure, an uneasy silence gripped the four women. Maria broke it by pushing heavily to her feet.

"You must eat, *Duquesa*. All of us must. I will make a frittata."

She swished through the swinging door to the kitchen, leaving Gina and the duchess to face a clearly worried Zia.

"I knew my brother had worked with Interpol," the Hungarian said with a deep crease between her brows, "but I was not aware he was…he was…" She waved a hand, as though trying to pull down the right word.

"An undercover agent?" Gina supplied.

"*Igen!* An undercover agent." Her accent reflected her agitation. The Eastern European rhythm grew more marked with each word. "Dominic never spoke of such things to me. Nor to our parents."

Gina wanted to believe her. Her aching chin dictated otherwise.

"He said last night he's no longer with Interpol," she reminded Zia coolly. "As I recall, he mentioned that he's now an independent entrepreneur. What, exactly, does that mean?"

Her cousin's eyes flashed. "I don't know. He has business all over. Many parts of the world. Something to do with security. But…I don't know."

She raked a hand through her silky black hair. She was dressed casually today in navy leggings and a belted, cream-colored tunic with a scoop neckline that dipped off one shoulder. Tall and slender and impossibly elegant, she stirred Gina's frumpy, dumpy feelings again.

Of course, it didn't help that she'd been in such a hurry to jump back into bed with Jack this morning that all she'd done in the bathroom was pee, splash her face with cold water and brush her teeth. Nor was her appearance uppermost in her mind when she'd come to. After her panicked 911 call, she'd scrambled into the same jeans and crab-apple stretchy T-shirt she'd worn last night. If she'd dragged a comb through her hair, she couldn't remember it. Makeup had never entered her mind. Aside from the ice pack Agent Driskell's partner had thrown together with a towel and minicubes from the wet bar to keep her jaw from swelling, Gina had given zero thought to how she looked.

She was feeling that omission now. She wanted a shower, a hairbrush, a change of clothes and another ice pack in the worst way. She hated to take the time for even a quick scrub, though. What if Agent Driskell called? Or Dom? Or Jack?

She was still debating the issue when Zia addressed the duchess. "This is very awkward for you," she said stiffly. "And for me. I think perhaps I should pack my things and… and Dom's…and go to a hotel."

The duchess frowned but before she could reply the cordless phone on the table beside her chair rang. Gina dived for it, praying fervently. Jack! Please, God, let it please be Jack!

"Hello?" Stabbing the talk button, she fumbled the receiver to her ear. "Hello?"

"Gina! Thank God!"

She had to strain to hear her sister's voice over the roar of some kind of engine.

"Grandmama called us early hours and hours ago," Sarah shouted above the noise. "She said you'd been in some kind of an incident. Are you okay?"

"I'm fine."

"The baby?"

Gina laid a hand over her still-flat stomach. Dom had caught her just as her knees crumpled. She hadn't hit the floor. Hadn't bruised anything but her chin. Which, she realized belatedly, must have been his intent.

"Also fine," she assured Sarah. "What's that noise? Where are you?"

"Just about to touch down at the 34th Street Heliport."

"You're here? In New York?"

"Dev ordered his private jet two minutes after Grandmama called. We'll be at the Dakota shortly. Gina, you're not hurt? You swear you're not hurt?"

"I swear."

"Okay, see you in a bit."

Gina cut the connection, battling the almost overwhelming urge to burst into tears. Dammit! These kamikaze hormones were killing her! But just knowing that the sister who always was and always would be her closest friend had rushed to New York on the basis of a single phone call made her want to bawl.

She fought back the tears and sent the duchess a tremulous smile. "That was Sarah."

"So I gathered. They're in New York?"

"They're about to touch down at the 34th Street Heliport."

Her grandmother's paper-thin eyelids fluttered down, as though in prayer. "Thank heavens."

When her lids lifted again, relief was stamped all across her face. "If anyone can get to the bottom of all this, Dev can."

Gina wasn't sure what her brother-in-law could do that two dozen assorted city, state and federal law officials couldn't. She'd put her money on Dev, though. He didn't have to play by the same rules those officials did.

"Now I must leave," Zia said, returning to the topic she'd introduced before the phone call. "Your other granddaughter comes, yes? You will need the bedroom for her."

"Why don't we wait until Sarah and Dev arrive before we decide that?" the duchess suggested.

Zia wasn't fooled. Neither was Gina. They both knew the duchess intended to keep their only connection to Dom on a short leash until Dev had a chance to talk to her.

Her cousin acknowledged as much with a curt nod. "Very well."

Then the stiffness went out of her spine. Like an elegant doll that suddenly lost its stuffing, Zia collapsed onto the sofa and put her head in her hands.

"Dominic is the best of all brothers," she said on a small moan. "I don't understand this. I don't understand any of this."

Her distress was so genuine, so obviously unfeigned. If Zia loved her brother even half as much as Gina loved Sarah, this crazy situation had to be tearing her apart.

The realization gave Gina more of a sense of kinship with her cousin than she'd felt at any point before. It brought her out of her chair and halfway across the sitting room before the buzz of the intercom sent her spinning toward the wall unit. The flashing number on the panel signaled a call from the lobby.

"It's Gina, Jerome."

"There's a gentleman to see you, Lady Eugenia. Mr. John Mason says…"

"Send him up!"

Thank God, thank God, thank God! Jack had returned from wherever he'd disappeared to.

She raced to the front door and flung it open. She was dancing from foot to foot in wild impatience when the elevator doors pinged open. Like a stork hit by lightning, she froze with one foot lifted in the air.

Jack's father stalked out of the elevator, his face red with suppressed fury. "What the hell have you involved my son in?"

Thirteen

She fell back a step, stunned by the vicious accusation. Before she could respond, before she could even think of a response, Zia came running down the hall.

"Come quickly! Special Agent Driskell's on the phone. She thinks they have a link to the kidnappers."

Gina spun on one heel and raced for the sitting room. Footsteps pounded behind her but she had no thought for Jack's father at the moment. Her heart pounding, she snatched up the phone the duchess held out and jammed it to her ear.

"This is Gina St. Sebastian. What's happening?"

"We just got a tip from Interpol," Pam Driskell said with barely suppressed excitement. "Antonio Cordi disappeared from their radar three days ago and may have entered the U.S. under a fake passport."

Like that told Gina anything!

"Who's Antonio Cordi?"

"He's the suspected capo of a vicious crime family operating out of southern Italy. Unfortunately, no one's been able to penetrate the family or get close enough to pin anything on him."

"You're kidding!" She gripped the phone with a white-knuckled fist. "What connection does Jack—Ambassador Mason—have to a Mafia don?"

A grim, white-faced John Harris Mason II surged into her field of view. "I can answer that."

Gina had the phone plastered against her ear, trying to assimilate John II's startling announcement, when she heard a commotion in the foyer. Her heart jumped into her throat.

Jack! Dom! Please God, let it be one of them!

She was hit with alternating waves of crushing disappointment and heartfelt joy when Sarah and Dev appeared. Waving a frantic hello, she relayed the latest development to Special Agent Driskell.

"Ambassador Mason's father is here at our apartment. He says he's got information about this Antonio Cordi."

"Keep him there! My partner and I are only a few blocks away. We'll return immediately."

Her thoughts whirling, Gina inserted the phone into its base. "Agent Driskell wants you to hang loose. She's on her way back here."

The thump of a cane against the parquet floor commanded her attention. "I believe introductions are in order, Eugenia."

"Oh. Right. Grandmama, Sarah, Dev, Zia…this is Jack's father, John Mason. John, this is my grandmother, sister, brother-in-law and…and cousin."

She hadn't intended the stumble over that last part. In her heart of hearts, Gina refused to believe Dom had gone over to the dark side. She still hadn't been able to come up with an explanation for his role in this morning's extraordinary events, though. Neither had his sister. Their unanswered questions hung over the room like a black cloud.

Zia acknowledged as much with a terse nod in the general direction of the newcomers. Which left Gina to pray the duchess hadn't heard the accusation flung at her by Jack's father in the hall a few moments ago. If Charlotte had, blood might yet be spilled.

Mason skated on that one, thank God. The duchess rose

from her chair with the aid of her ebony cane and held out a blue-veined hand.

"I'm sorry we have to meet under such unhappy circumstances, John. I may call you John, mightn't I?"

He gave a curt nod, his thoughts obviously spinning more on his son than on social niceties.

"Good, and you may call me Charlotte. Now, please, sit down and tell us what connection your son has to a Mafia don."

Mason a dismissive gesture with one hand. "I'll wait for the FBI."

Gina chalked the rudeness up to the worry that had to be gnawing at him but cringed at the expression his brush-off put on her grandmother's face.

"Gina says this FBI agent is on the way to take my statement. I'll wait and..."

"No, sir, you will not."

The duchess's cane whipped up and took aim at his chest.

"Look at that bruise on my granddaughter's chin," she commanded with icy hauteur. "If you have an explanation for why her cousin felt compelled to strike her and disappear into thin air with your son, I want to hear it. Now."

Gina guessed John II rarely, if ever, tucked his tail between his legs and backed off. He didn't exactly do either at that point, but he offered a stiff reply.

"I can't tell you why this...this cousin of Gina's struck her or how *he's* involved in this situation. I have my suspicions," he said, his jaw tight, "but nothing solid to base them on. All I can tell you is that I once headed a delegation chartered to examine international banking practices that shielded money laundering, both in the U.S. and abroad. We spent months in South America, more months in Europe digging into accounts reputedly owned by an Italian crime organization called the 'Ndrangheta."

"Go on," the duchess instructed as she resumed her seat. "And for heaven's sake, do sit down."

The demand for at least a semblance of normality drained the last of John II's hostility. He sank into a chair, looking suddenly haggard and far older than his years.

Gina and Sarah and Zia huddled together on the sofa. Dev took the straight-backed chair at the duchess's gilt-edged escritoire. Every pair of eyes was locked on Jack's father as he reduced what had to be a dramatic tale of international crime and intrigue to a few, stark sentences.

"We were in Rome. With the help of the Italian authorities, we'd actually begun to decipher the labyrinthine flow of third- and fourth-tier transactions. One of those tiers led to a member of the 'Ndrangheta named Francesco Cordi."

"I thought his name was Antonio," Gina said, frowning.

"Francesco is—was—Antonio's brother.

"Was?"

"Francesco's dead."

John scrubbed a hand over his face. It was evident to everyone in the room he still carried vivid memories of those days in Rome.

"He didn't like us nosing around in his business and decided to let us know about it. Two of my associates were incinerated when their vehicle was firebombed. We found out later I was next on the hit list. Fortunately—or unfortunately as it now turns out—Jack flew over to Rome at the first sign of trouble. He was with me when Francesco made his move." A fleeting smile creased the retired diplomat's face. "There wasn't a whole lot left of him to send home to his brother Antonio."

"Who's now here, in the States," Gina explained for Sarah and Dev. "The FBI says they got a tip that…"

The buzz of the intercom had her springing her off the sofa.

"That must be Agent Driskell and her partner now."

It wasn't. Her stomach sank like a stone when Jerome announced another visitor.

"I'm sorry to bother you, Lady Eugenia, but there's a Mr. Dale Vickers in the lobby."

Jack's obnoxious chief of staff. That's all she needed! Squeezing her eyes shut, Gina pressed her forehead against the wall.

"He wishes to speak with you. Shall I send him up?"

Hell, no! She knew darn well the officious little turd possessed no vital information relating to his boss's kidnapping. If he had, he would have taken it straight to the FBI. She would also bet he'd already used the weight of his office to extract every detail he could from them. Now he wanted to hear it straight from the horse's mouth.

She guessed she couldn't blame him. Vickers and Jack went back a long way. He had to be as shaken as everyone in the room. Sighing, Gina raised her head.

"Send him up."

Mere moments after the short, tightly wired Vickers said hello to Jack's father and was introduced to others, he confirmed Gina's cynical guess. The man had spoken to just about every local, state and federal official involved into the case.

"They can't tell me a damned thing beyond the basics. All they could confirm was that you and the ambassador were screwing around when he got snatched and…"

"Stop right there, young man!"

Incensed, the duchess tilted her chin to a dangerous angle.

"You will address Lady Eugenia with courtesy and respect or you will leave this apartment immediately."

"I…"

"Do we understand each other?"

"I just…"

"A simple 'yes, ma'am' will do."

"Yes, ma'am."

Despite the tension engulfing the room, Gina and Sarah exchanged a small smile. The sisters had seen their grandmother reduce bigger and stronger men than Dale Vickers to quivering blobs of sorry.

Vickers's next comment erased any inclination to smile, however. Too wired to accept the duchess's icily polite invitation to have a seat, he paced the sitting room.

"I know it was clutching at straws, but I even thought this might have something to do with the face-to-face between the ambassador and the CEO of Global Protective Services at that little soiree TTG put on last weekend."

Little soiree? Gina swallowed an indignant huff. She had to work hard to refrain from suggesting Vickers take a short leap off a tall building.

Unaware he'd ignited her fuse, the staffer proceeded to send her straight into orbit. "If Global's power structure thought the ambassador was going to undercut them on the fat embassy security contract they're trying to land, they might want him out of the picture. When I called Nikki, though, she assured me…"

"Whoa! Back up a minute. Did you just say you called Nikki?" Gina asked incredulously. "Nicole Tremayne? My boss?"

"Of course I called her. She appreciates the business we've sent TTG's way since you and the ambassador…uh…" He caught the duchess's warning glance. "Since you and the ambassador started seeing each other. But I knew she didn't understand the awkward position you put him in by enticing him to attend an event sponsored by Global."

Gina barely heard the last, insulting remark. She was still dealing with the shock of learning that Jack and his staff had funneled business to TTG.

Her pride crumbled. Like an old, rotted rowboat, it just fell apart right before her eyes. What a fool she was! All these weeks she'd thought, she'd actually believed, she was making her own mark at TTG.

She struggled to her feet. She refused to burst into tears in front of Vickers, but her throat was thick when she reminded the assembled group that Special Agent Driskell and her partner were expected at any moment.

"Sarah, would you show them in when they get here? I need to... I need to..."

She didn't trust herself to finish. With a vague gesture toward the arched hallway leading to the rear of the apartment, she turned on her heel. Her eyes were burning by the time she made it the bath linking her bedroom with Sarah's old room. She dropped the lid to the stool and sank down sideways, crossing both arms on the counter beside it.

Strangely, the tears didn't gush. Gina stared at the wall, her pride in shreds, and waited for the usual flood to burst through the dam. It took a moment for her to understand why the tsunami didn't happen.

None of it mattered. Not her job or TTG or Vickers's snide comments. The *only* thing that mattered right now was Jack's safety. She would eat crow or humble pie or black, slimy worms if that would bring him back to her.

She was still staring blankly at the wall when Sarah tapped on the bathroom door.

"Gina? Are you okay?"

"Mostly."

"May I come in?"

She mumbled an assent and almost lost it when her sister eased down onto her knees beside the stool. Gina had counted on Sarah to bail her out of so many of life's little catastrophes. Turned to her, too, to soothe the ruffled feathers of the men she'd fallen for, then dropped with such careless abandon.

"It'll be okay," Sarah murmured, stroking her hair. "It'll be okay. Judging by everything I've heard in the past few minutes, Jack's been in tight spots before. He'll find a way out of this one, too."

Halfway across town Jack was was hungry, hurting and totally pissed.

He'd been sitting on his ass for hours now in a wobbly

chair with one leg shorter than the other. His arms were twisted behind his back. Plastic restraints cut into his wrists. The wound from the bullet that had grazed his upper arm had scabbed over, but the trail of dried blood it left itched like the devil under the shirt and suit coat he'd been told to pull on before they'd departed his hotel suite.

Jack had complied with the order. Hell, with Dominic St. Sebastian cradling an unconscious Gina in his arms, Jack would have jumped out the eighth-story window if so ordered to prevent the bastard from hurting her any worse.

He'd had time these past hours to think about that, though. How fast St. Sebastian had put himself between Gina and his two pals with guns. How quickly he'd clipped her, then caught her before she hit the floor. As though he wanted to neutralize her and get her out of the picture immediately, before the other goons turned their weapons in her direction.

If so, he hadn't bothered to communicate his strategy to Jack. Or anything else, for that matter. St. Sebastian and the shorter of his two pals had disappeared right after they'd dumped Jack in this abandoned warehouse.

They'd left the shaved-head Goliath to stand guard. The giant had heaved his bulk up twice in the past six hours, both times to take a leak. He'd sprayed the grimy brick wall like a fire hose, adding his contribution to the stench of vomit, urine and rat feces littering what was obviously a hangout for homeless druggies. He'd also grunted into a cell phone a few times in a heavy dialect Jack couldn't understand but otherwise refused to say a word.

Shifting in his chair to ease the ache in his shoulder joints, Jack decided to take another shot at him. "Hey! Num nuts! I know you won't respond to English."

He tried Spanish again, then French, then his limited Russian. All he got was a sneer and a shake of the thug's massive head.

Okay. All right. Jack couldn't wait any longer. If the nine or ten layers of local, state and federal officials he knew had to be looking for him hadn't closed in on the warehouse by now, odds were pretty damned good they wouldn't. If Jack were going to get out of this mess, he had to do it on his own.

For the fifth or sixth time he did a visual sweep of the warehouse. Rat droppings weren't the only objects littering its dim, cavernous interior. A stained mattress, some moldy fast-food sacks and a scatter of rusted tin cans gave ample evidence of prior occupation. So did the syringes dropped on the concrete floor.

His glance lingered on the syringes. He'd considered those earlier but the damned things were plastic, not glass. Even if he could toe one within reach, somehow get it into his hands and break the barrel before the gorilla noticed, the plastic shard wouldn't cut through the restraints.

He'd have to go with a rusted can. The closest was about four feet away. Its lid was jagged and bent back, as though someone had used an old-fashioned can opener to get at the contents, then tossed it aside.

He couldn't wiggle the rickety chair that far without getting Goliath all excited. He had to take a dive. Probably more than one. He just hoped to hell he didn't knock himself unconscious when he hit the cement floor.

"Hey! You!"

Goliath slewed a disinterested glance Jack's way.

"I need to take a leak, too."

Hard to pantomime without the use of your arms. He tipped his chin toward his fly. When that didn't produce results, he nodded toward the urine-splashed wall, arced his arms behind him to clear the chair and started to push to his feet.

His guard grunted a warning. Jack ignored it. He was almost upright when the giant lunged out of his own chair and swung the beefy fist gripping his silenced semiautomatic.

The blow knocked Jack sideways. He crashed to the cement. The rickety chair went with him. Goliath said something that was obviously a warning and hooked a paw under

Jack's arm. Of course, he had to grab the one grazed by the bullet.

When Jack grimaced in pain, amusement lit Goliath's broad, flat face. He muttered a few words that no doubt translated to "serves you right, asshole" and righted the overturned chair. He shoved Jack into it and headed back to his own.

"I have to piss."

His jaw set, Jack started to rise again. And again, Goliath let fly with a backhanded blow. And this time, he couldn't be bothered to right the chair or haul his hostage up into it.

Jack's lips curled in a snarl. His eyes never left the gorilla's. Muttering profanities that only seemed to increase the big man's amusement, he got a grip on the rusted can he'd landed almost on top of. He maneuvered it with his fingertips until he turned the jagged lid inward. As he surreptitiously sawed at the plastic restraints, he wondered fleetingly how long it had been since his last tetanus shot. No matter. Lockjaw was the least of his worries right now. His gut told him Dominic St. Sebastian's pals played for keeps.

He got confirmation of that just moments after the giant's cell phone buzzed. Goliath picked up the instrument, glanced at the number displayed on the screen and hit Talk. Two grunts later, he set the phone down. A few moments after that, a door at the far end of the warehouse opened.

Still lying on his side, Jack curved his body so his front faced the door and his wrists were hidden behind his back. The damned can lid was slippery with blood from slicing into his skin, but the grim realization that it was now or never kept him razoring at the restraints.

He also kept his eyes on the three men who came through the door. One he recognized from the hotel. The second was a stranger. The third was Dominic St. Sebastian. His features seemed to freeze when he spotted the body sprawled on the concrete. Then his eyes caught Jack's. He flashed a swift, silent message, but before Jack could interpret that damned thing, the stranger took a wide-legged stance a few yards away. He was dressed in a sleek gray suit and white wing tips. A distant corner of Jack's mind was wondering who the hell wore wing tips anymore when a vicious smile cut across the man's swarthy face.

"I have waited a long time for this, Ambassador."

"That right?"

"I thought to take you in Washington, but security there is too tight. How convenient that you have a woman here in New York."

The jagged lid took another slice out of Jack's thumb. He couldn't work the lid too hard with the stranger's eyes on him, but he didn't give up.

"Convenient for you, maybe," he drawled. "Not so much for me. Who the hell are you, anyway?"

"I am Antonio Cordi, the brother of Francesco Cordi. Perhaps you remember him?"

"Yeah, I remember him. Hard to forget the man who tried to gun down my father."

"And failed, unfortunately. We don't often miss our targets."

"'We' being you and the other scumbags who comprise 'Ndrangheta."

Jack was all too familiar with the confederation of Italian families that rose to power after the Cosa Nostra's decline in the 1990s. By forming alliances with Central and South American drug cartels, 'Ndrangheta had gone global and was now one of the world's most powerful criminal organizations. Its members were up to their hairy armpits in drug trafficking, prostitution, extortion, weapons smuggling and kidnappings for ransom. One U.S. State Department white paper estimated that their illegal activities accounted for more than $43 billion in 2007 alone—or approximately three percent of Italy's total gross domestic product.

Jack had gotten up close and personal with only one member of the clan, when his dad had been tapped to lead a delegation exploring the extent to which the 'Ndrangheta's money laundering had infiltrated the international banking system. The delegation followed one of the links to Francesco Cordi. When they dug a little too deep, Cordi retaliated by going after the high-ranking members of the delegation. Two died when their car was firebombed. Jack flew to Rome as soon as he heard about it and was with his father when Cordi came after him.

He had no regrets about taking Cordi down. Not then, not now. Even though he'd been advised by several concerned Italian officials that every member of the 'Ndrangheta swore a blood oath to always, *always* avenge the death of one of their own.

So he wasn't surprised when Cordi's brother slid a hand inside the jacket of his pearl-gray suit. Or that the hand emerged holding a blue steel Beretta.

Fourteen

Gina had never been inside a military command post but she suspected they couldn't be any more crowded or more tense than the apartment once Special Agent Driskell and her partner arrived.

With the duchess's permission, the FBI agents commandeered the study to interview Jack's father in private. That left Gina, her grandmother, Sarah, Dev, Zia and the obnoxious Dale Vickers to pick at the buffet lunch Maria had miraculously managed to augment with the arrival of each new wave of visitors.

Gina re-ee-eally wanted to tell Vickers to find somewhere else to squat, but the man was so worried about his friend and boss she didn't have the heart to kick him out of their unofficial command center. Besides, he and Dev seemed to have formed an unlikely partnership.

She tried to set aside her animosity for Vickers and study the two men objectively as they sat across from her, with the remains of the buffet lunch still littering the table. Jack's chief of staff was in an expensive-looking suit with his tie loosened and the top button of his shirt popped. Dev wore jeans and a faded, light blue denim shirt with the sleeves rolled up. With his broad shoulders, close-cropped black hair and tanned skin, he looked as if he spent more time on his parents' New Mexico ranch than in boardrooms all around the globe. Yet anyone looking at the two men could easily pick out the power broker. Dev Hunter exuded the utter confidence that came with having built a multinational aerospace corporation from the ground up.

"Are you sure Jack had his cell phone on him when he left Washington?" he asked Vickers.

"I'm sure."

Frowning, Dev worked the buttons of his handheld device. "It's not emitting a signal."

"I could have told you that," Gina said. "Someone..."

She scrunched her forehead and ran through a mental litany of officials who'd responded to her 911 call. The NYPD detectives? The guy from the counterterrorism office? Pam Driskell? Aside from the short, stocky FBI agent, they were all pretty much a nameless, faceless blur now.

"I can't remember who, but someone ran a trace on Jack's cell phone within moments of showing up at the Excelsior. Maybe several someones. They said any recently manufactured cell phone has a built-in tracking device that allows eavesdroppers to pinpoint its location to within just a few feet."

"Unless the battery is removed," Dev muttered, playing with his gizmo. "Which must be the case here, or the ultra high frequency cargo container signal receptor we're developing for MilSatCom would pick it up."

"The what for the who?"

"I can't speak to the 'what,'" Sarah said as Dev continued to scowl at the instrument in his hand, "but the 'who' is the Military Satellite Communications System."

When both the duchess and Gina turned to stare at her, she smiled at their look of astonishment. "Don't be so surprised. I've been receiving a crash course on all things military since we got back from our honeymoon."

"You're serious?"

"As serious as the self-contained, bolt-on/bolt-off special operations surveillance system mounted in the belly of a C-130," she said solemnly.

Gina tried, she really tried, to picture her oh-so-elegant sister in one of the retro designer classic outfits she loved clambering around the belly of a C-130. Not that Gina knew what a C-130 was, exactly.

"What about your brother?" Dev asked Zia, cutting into Gina's wild imaginings. "Do you know Dom's cell phone number?"

"Of course," she said wearily. "But the police ran a trace on that, too, with no results."

"With all due respect to our various law enforcement agencies, they don't yet have access to the kind of technology I'm talking about here. It's still in the developmental stage and... Well, damn! That's it!"

Dev's exclamation shot up the tension level among the others in the room. The women all sat up in their chairs. Vickers hunched closer as Dev whipped out his own cell phone.

"That's what?" Vickers asked.

Shaking his head in obvious self-disgust, Dev tapped a number on his speed dial. "Why the hell didn't I think of it before?"

"Think of what?"

"Hold on." He put the phone to his ear. "Pat, I need the MilSat access code for the gamma version of CSR-II. I've been trying to get on using the beta version but... Yeah, I know. I know. Just get me the damned code."

"Ooooh," Sarah murmured, her green eyes dancing, "that's going to cost him."

"Pat Donovan is Dev's right-hand man," Gina explained to a bewildered Zia. "He's a wizard. Really, I think the man has magical powers. He can move mountains with a single phone call."

"If not mountains, at least the occupants of an entire Parisian hotel," Sarah recalled. "I don't know what kind of a bonus Dev paid him for that particular trick but I have a feeling it ran to big bucks."

"Say again," Dev barked into the phone, his brows knit. "Right. Right. Okay, got it. What? Yeah, we'll talk about that later."

He disconnected and switched to his handheld device. The thing looked so innocuous. Just a small, wafer-thin box with a greenish-colored digital screen and a set of icons that appeared with the tap of a finger. It fit in the palm of Dev's hand and could easily be mistaken for a smart phone, except this little gadget could evidently bounce signals off the moon or something.

He was entering a long involved code when the sliding doors to the study slammed back. Every head turned in surprise as Driskell's partner raced out and made a beeline for the foyer. Driskell herself was right on his heels, with Jack's dad staggering white-faced behind them.

The FBI agent paused only long enough to throw out a terse explanation. "We've got a report of shots fired. Initial indications are the situation may involve the ambassador."

"Involve *how?*" Gina jumped up. The violent movement sent her chair crashing to the floor. "Agent Driskell, wait! Is Jack hurt?"

"Or my brother?" Zia demanded as she, too, surged to her feet.

"I don't know," the FBI agent replied on the run. "I'll contact y'all as soon as I do."

"I'm coming with you!"

Gina shouted to an empty space. Driskell was already out the front door, leaving a frozen tableau of tension and fear in her wake. Dev shattered the silence with an abrupt command.

"Gina, do you have Driskell's cell phone number?"

She could hardly speak past the terror lodged like a spiked ball in her throat. "Yes."

Wedging a hand into the pocket of her jeans, she extracted

the business card Driskell had given her earlier. Dev snatched it from her fingers and entered the number on his device. Mere seconds later, his blue eyes lit with fierce satisfaction.

"Okay, I've got her." He swung toward the foyer. "Let's go."

Gina, Zia, Jack's dad and Dale Vickers all wheeled in a swift formation that would have done a platoon of marines proud. Their syncopated turn didn't impress Dev.

"Whoa! We can't all—"

"Do not say it!" Zia interrupted. Her dark eyes blazed and her accent went thick with passion. "I am a doctor. If Dom… If anyone is hurt, I can help."

"I'm going, too," Jack's dad growled.

Dale Vickers didn't say a thing but his pugnacious expression dared anyone, Dev included, to try and stop him.

Sarah was the only who exhibited any restraint. "I'll stay with Grandmama." Her gaze drilled into her husband. "But please, please, be careful."

"I will." Dev strode for the foyer. "We'll have to take two cabs."

"Sarah!" Gina called over her shoulder. "Buzz down and tell Jerome to get on his whistle. We need two taxis, like pronto!"

The doorman had them lined up and waiting at the curb when they all poured out of the elevators. Dev aimed for the lead vehicle and issued orders in a voice that said he wasn't allowing vetoes this time.

"Gina, you and Zia with me. Vickers, you follow with Mr. Mason."

They scrambled into their assigned cabs. Gina and Zia took the backseat of the first, Dev folded his tall frame into the front.

"Hey, mon," the cabbie said in a lilting Caribbean accent that matched his shoulder-length dreadlocks and colorful orange, green, yellow and black knit cap. "Where ya goin'?"

"Straight down Central Park West until I tell you to turn."

The cabbie shrugged and activated his meter. As the leafy green of the park zipped by, Dev kept his narrowed gaze on the street grid filling his screen.

Gina edged forward on her seat and looked over his shoulder. All she could see was a tiny red dot racing along the grid.

"Is that Driskell?"

"It is."

"What happens if she gets or makes a call? You won't lose the track, will you?"

"Heads in my R-and-D division will roll if I do."

Not quite reassured by that grim prediction, Gina groped for her cousin's hand. Zia threw her a glance filled with equal parts hope and determination.

"They will be okay, your man and my brother. But to make sure…" She squeezed Gina's fingers. "I shall say a special prayer to Saint Stephen. He is the patron saint of your grandmother's homeland, you know."

No, Gina didn't know. At this point, though, she would pray to any celestial being who might intercede on Jack and Dom's behalf.

As if sensing how close her cousin was to a total meltdown, Zia tried to distract her with details about the saint. "He is Istvan in our language. He was born in 965 or '67 or '75. No one knows for sure. His father was Grand Prince Géza of Hungary. His mother, the daughter of Gylua of Transylvania."

The mention of Transylvania diverted Gina long enough for all-too-vivid images of werewolves springing out of coffins to flash into her mind. Or was it vampires who rose from the dead? For God's sake! Who cared?

Zia refused to let her cousin's wildly careening thoughts and emotions overwhelm her. Speaking calmly, slowly, soothingly, she related how the eventual Saint Istvan married Giselle of Bavaria and ascended to the throne of the Magyars on the death of his father. How he discouraged pagan customs and strengthened Christianity by a series of strict laws. How he was devastated by the death of his oldest son, Emeric, in a hunting accident, after which his cousin, Duke Vazul, took part in an assassination conspiracy.

"The attempt failed," Zia related as Dev issued a sharp order to the cabbie to cut across town. "Vazul had his eyes gouged out and molten lead poured in his ears."

"Umm," Gina murmured.

Her eyes were on that blinking red dot, her thoughts anywhere but with some long dead saint.

"Without a living heir, King St. Istvan asked the Blessed Virgin Mary to take the Hungarian people as her subjects and become their queen. He died on the same feast day that commemorates the assumption into heaven of the Blessed Virgin Mary, yes?"

"What? Oh. Right."

Gina had no idea what her cousin had been talking about. Her focus was on the bridge ahead. As a native New Yorker, she understood why the cabbie balked.

"I don't do runs to that part of Brooklyn," he said with a head shake that set his dreadlocks swinging.

"There's an extra five hundred in it for you," Dev countered.

"Say no more, mon."

As they cruised onto the bridge, Gina twisted around. The second cab was still following. She dropped back in her seat, wondering how much Jack's dad had offered his driver.

Once across the bridge they entered a twilight zone of abandoned warehouses and crumbling industrial facilities. The area had formerly been home to the Brooklyn Navy Yard and had died a painful death in the '60s or '70s. Gina knew a comeback was planned, but it was still a ways off.

Artists and commercial activities rented space in the cavernous building that hadn't collapsed under the weight of time and disuse. She saw a bright pink neon sign indicating a movie studio. Another, slightly less attention-grabbing bill-board advertised Brooklyn Grange Farm. The farm suppos-edly utilized 45,000 square feet on the roof of Building 3, wherever that was. Sadly, all too many of the structures showed an endless vista of graffiti-covered walls, trash-strewn yards fenced off with razor wire, and row after row of broken windows.

With every deserted block the cab skimmed past, Gina's hopes dipped lower and lower. They hit rock-bottom when the taxi turned a corner and she spotted what looked like twenty or more emergency vehicles dead ahead.

The cabbie screeched to a halt a half block away. "Hey, mon, I can't cruise close to no cop cars. They might have dogs with 'em."

"Christ," Dev muttered, "what are you hauling in... Oh, hell, never mind."

He shoved a wad of bills at the driver and shouldered open the door. Gina and Zia scrambled out at the same time.

"Stay here until I scope out the situation," Dev ordered brusquely.

"No way," Gina said, her frantic gaze locked on the two ambulances parked side by side amid the other vehicles.

She took off after Zia, who'd already broken into a dead run. All Dev could do at that point was curse and charge after her. If shots were fired from any of the broken windows star-ing sightlessly down at them, he'd damned well better get in front of Gina and shield her body with his. Sarah would never forgive him if her sister got hurt. Zia would just have to take her chances.

The cabbie barely waited for them to clear his vehicle be-fore screeching into a three-point turn. He almost swiped the second cab's fender when he peeled off. Dev heard the shriek of brakes, the thud of doors slamming, the slam of footsteps on pavement as Vickers and Jack's father raced down the street.

Luckily, they all reached the protective screen of emergency vehicles without shots erupting from the warehouse. The uniformed officer on the perimeter looked as if he might draw his weapon, though, when the two women leading the charge ignored his command to stop. Parting like the proverbial Red Sea, they started to go around him.

"Hey! Hold it right there."

He made a grab for the closest, which happened to be Zia, and got a face full of raging female.

"*Vagyok orvos!* Ach! I am doctor! Doctor!"

Her unleashed emotions made her accent so heavy that the English was almost indistinguishable from the Hungarian. Neither made an impression on the uniformed officer.

"Look, lady, you…all of you…better not take another friggin' step until I see some ID, log you in and get clearance to…"

"*Ide,* Anastazia!"

The shout came from an unmarked vehicle parked inside the cordon. Zia whirled and gave a glad cry. The rest of the group spun around, as well. Gina registered a half-dozen wildly careening thoughts as she watched Dominic stride toward them.

Blood seeped from a slash high on one cheek. One eye was swollen shut. He wasn't in handcuffs. And he was alone.

Dear God! He was alone.

With a sob of sheer terror, she dodged the uniformed officer and broke into another run. He gave a shout, but interpreted a short air-chop from Dominic as a signal that his duty lay in keeping the rest of the crowd corralled.

Ten steps later, Gina flung herself at Dominic. Her fists hammered a frantic drumbeat on his chest. "Where's Jack? What did you do with him? If you or those thugs you were with hurt him, I'll carve out your heart and shove it down your throat."

Dom's eyes widened, and Gina shocked even herself with the viciousness of the threat. A distant corner of her mind registered a flicker of surprise that she hadn't burst into her by-now-usual flood of tears. Her otherwise volatile hormones seemed to have narrowed to a single, deadly and completely primal urge.

If this man—if any man—had harmed her mate, she'd make that Italian crime organization Jack's dad mentioned seem like a bunch of playful kindergarteners.

"Tell me, dammit. Where's Jack?"

Dom caught her pounding fists before they did serious damage to his chest wall. "He's there, Gina." Keeping a careful grip on her wrists, he angled her around. "Talking with some agents from the FBI."

She spotted him the same moment he followed Agent Driskell's nod and glanced over his shoulder. In the ten seconds it took for Gina to wrestle out of Dom's hold and Jack to sprint the fifty or so yards separating them, she saw that he was as bruised as her cousin.

But it was his eyes that lit her heart up like the Fourth of July. His fierce, unguarded expression. The raw, male pheromones shooting off him like live sparks when he caught her in his arms. Her blood singing with joy, she returned his kiss with every ounce of relief, of desire, of love that was in her.

Swift, frightening sanity came in the form of a sticky residue that transferred from the sleeve of his dark charcoal suit coat to Gina's palm. In her mad rush to his arms, she hadn't noticed the stain.

She couldn't miss it now. It left her palm a rusty red and a lump of dismay the size of a basketball bouncing around in her stomach. Gently, gingerly, she tried to ease away from the injured arm.

"You're hurt."

"So are you."

He curled a knuckle under her chin and angled her chin to survey the ugly bruise.

"I thought slamming my fist into your cousin's eye made up for this," he said, murder in his voice. "Looks like he still has some payment coming."

"You gave Dom his black eye?" Gina couldn't make sense of any of this. "If he was part of the plot to kidnap you, why isn't he under arrest?"

"Long story. Why don't we...?" He broke off, his gaze going to the men who now approached. "Hello, Dad. Dale."

Jack didn't seem the least surprised to see his father or chief of staff. Gina backed away to give them access to the man they all loved. She could share him with his family. With his obnoxious assistant. With his memories of Catherine.

And with the child they would welcome to the world in just a few short months. Lost in a love undiminished by the past or constrained by the present, Gina acknowledged there was more than enough of Jack Mason to go around.

Fifteen

Once again the duchess's spacious apartment served as command central. Most of the key players in the day's drama sat elbow-to-elbow at the dining table, relieving their tension with their choice of coffee, iced tea, fruit juice, *žuta osa* or the last of the double-distilled *pálinka*.

The duchess and Jack's father had opted for the brandy. Jack, Dev, Zia and Dom braved the throat-searing kick of the liqueur. Dale Vickers went with coffee, while Gina and Sarah chose juice. The duchess insisted Maria fill her own glass rather than trying to keep everyone's topped off and just sit down.

Pam Driskell put in a brief appearance, as did Jerome. The doorman had delegated his post to a subordinate to accompany the FBI agent upstairs. He'd abandoned his dignity long enough to wrap Gina in a fierce hug. He then shook Jack's hand, told him how happy he was to see him safe and went back to work.

The only major players who failed to put in an appearance were Antonio Cordi and his two thugs. Cordi because he was dead, shot through the heart during the violence that erupted inside the warehouse just moments before the police arrived. One of his hired hands was also deceased, the big one Jack bitingly referred to as Goliath. He'd had his jugular sliced by the lid of a rusty tin can and had bled out before the EMTs arrived. The second thug was now a guest of the U.S. government and likely to remain so for a long, long time.

Even now, huddled at the table that could seat twenty comfortably with the leaves in, Gina felt sick at the thought of how close both Jack and Dom had been to being on the receiving end of a bullet.

"Cordi must have wondered if my well-publicized departure from Interpol was a blind," Dom related after tossing back another restorative shot of *pálinka*. "He allowed me into the outer fringe of 'Ndrangheta but never let me get close enough to gather the evidence we needed to nail him."

"So to get close to the capo," Jack drawled, "you suggested using your kinship to Gina as a means to get to me."

"Cordi had sworn a blood oath to avenge his brother," Dom said with an unrepentant shrug. "He would have gotten to you eventually. I merely proved my loyalty by offering to set up the hit."

Gina still couldn't believe the tangled web of lies and deceit Dom had lived for almost a year. Danger had stalked him with every breath, every step.

Zia was even more appalled. She'd had no idea her brother had infiltrated one of Europe's most vicious crime organizations. Or that he'd arranged this "business" trip to New York City for a specific, and very deadly, purpose.

"No wonder you balked at my decision to accompany you," she said, scowling.

"You would not have accompanied me, had I not been sure I could keep you safe from danger."

"Not to mention," Dev guessed shrewdly, "the fact that she added to your credibility with the duchess."

"Yes, there was that consideration." A wry smile curved Dom's lips. "You don't know my sister very well, however, if you think my objections carried any weight with her. If I hadn't been certain I could keep her safe, I would have been forced to chain her to a wall in the dungeon of the crumbling castle the Duchess Charlotte once called home."

Jack's voice cut across the table like a serrated knife blade. "Too bad you couldn't offer the same guarantees for Gina."

"Ah, yes."

Dom's glance went to the bruise on Gina's chin. His one eye was still swollen shut, but the other showed real chagrin. "I very much regret having to hurt you, cousin. My associates had become impatient, you see, and I had to act or risk blowing my cover."

His glance slewed to Jack, then back to Gina. A rakish glint replaced the regret in his good eye. "If you would but let me," he murmured, "I would kiss away the hurt."

Jack answered that. This time his tone was slow and lazy but even more lethal. "You really do like living on the edge, don't you, St. Sebastian?"

"That's enough!"

The sharp reprimand turned every head to the duchess. Her chin had tilted to a degree that both Gina and Sarah recognized instantly, and her faded blue eyes shot daggers at the two combatants.

"May I remind you that you're guests in my home? Dominic, you will cease making such deliberately provocative comments. Jack, you will stop responding like a Neanderthal ready to club all rivals. Gina…"

When her gimlet gaze zinged to her youngest granddaughter, Gina jerked upright in her chair. She'd been on the receiving end of that stare too many times to take it lightly.

"What did I do?"

"It's what you haven't done," the duchess informed her. "For pity's sake, tell Jack you love him as much as he so obviously loves you and get on with planning your wedding."

A few moments of stark silence greeted the acerbic pronouncement. Jack broke it with a cool reply. "With all due respect, Duchess, that's something Gina and I should discuss in private."

His father joined the fray with a sudden and explosive exclamation. "Bull hockey!"

"Dad…"

John II ignored his son's warning glance. The face he turned to Gina wore a mix of regret and resolution. "I know I acted like an ass when you came to visit us at Five Oaks."

"Pretty much," she agreed politely.

"I need to apologize for that. And for the ugly name I called you earlier this morning," he added with a wince.

"Christ, Dad, what the hell did you…?"

"Be quiet, Jack. This is between Gina and me."

John Harris Mason II hadn't lost his bite. His son matched him glower for glower but yielded the floor. Once again, the older man addressed Gina.

"That was unforgivable. I hope you'll chalk it up to a father sick to death with worry over his son."

"Consider it chalked," she said with a shaky smile.

Oh, boy! Her emotions were starting one of their wild swings. Now that the danger to Jack had passed and she was surrounded by everyone she loved most in the world, she wasn't sure how long she could hold out before dissolving into wet, sloppy tears.

Jack's father didn't help matters. He leaned forward, his gaze holding hers. "I've never seen anyone turn Jack on his head the way you have, Gina."

"Is that…?" She gulped. "Is that good?"

"Oh, yes. More than I can say. You've shaken him out of the mold I tried… We all tried," he said with a glance at Dale Vickers, "to force him into."

He paused. His throat worked, sending his Adam's apple up and down a few times. When he could speak again, his voice was raw with emotion.

"Jack's mother would be proud to call you daughter. So would I."

That did it. Gina could feel her face getting all blotchy with the effort of holding back tears. "I…I…"

Shoving back her chair, she resorted to her most trust-worthy excuse for beating an instant retreat.

"I have to pee."

Sarah had followed her when she'd retreated to the bath-room earlier in the afternoon. This time it was Jack. Except he didn't knock, as her sister had. Nor did he ask for per-mission to enter. He just barged in and kicked the door shut behind him.

Luckily, Gina hadn't really needed to go. Her panties weren't around her ankles. The skinny jeans she'd been wear-ing for what now felt like two lifetimes were still zipped up. She was on the pot, though, and the tears she'd tried so hard to stem streamed down her cheeks. Like Sarah, Jack sank to his knees beside the stool. Unlike Sarah, he didn't hesitate to drag Gina off the throne and into his arms.

"Don't cry, sweetheart. Please, don't cry."

He held her, rocking back and forth, while the residual stress and tension and fear poured out via her tear ducts.

"It's…it's the hormones," she said through hiccuping sobs. "I never cry. Never! Ask Sarah. Ask…ask Grandmama. They'll tell you."

"It's okay."

"Noooo," she wailed, "it's not."

She grabbed the front of his shirt. His bloodied shirt. He hadn't had time to change, either.

"I didn't get a chance to tell you this morning, Jack. I…I didn't think I'd ever get a chance to tell you. I love you."

"I know, darling."

"No, you don't!"

The tears evaporated, replaced by an urgency that reached deep into her core.

"I think…" She shook her head. "Scratch that! I know I fell a little bit in love with you our first weekend together. I'm not sure when I tumbled all the rest of the way, but I'm all the way there."

"Me, too, my darling."

His smile was all Jack. Charming, roguish and so damned sexy Gina could feel her tears drying and another part of her starting to get wet.

"So what do you think?" he said, dropping a kiss on her nose. "Want get off the floor, go back into the dining room and tell your grandmother to start planning a wedding?"

"No."

His confidence took a hit, but he recovered fast. Shaking his head, he acknowledged his gaffe. "I'm such a jackass. How could I forget you're the world's greatest event coordinator?"

"Yeah, right."

Those damned hormones! Gina could for the sneer curled her lip and the sulky response she couldn't hold back.

"I can't be that great if you had to send Washington business TTG's way."

"What are you talking about?"

"Dale told me you steered business to TTG." She made a heroic effort to keep the hurt out of her voice. "I appreciate it, Jack. I really do. It's just that I wanted to… I was trying to… Oh, crap!"

The hand that took her chin and tilted it up was anything but gentle.

"Listen to me, Eugenia Amalia Therése St. Sebastian. I'm going to say this once, and once only. If Dale Vickers or anyone else in my office steered business to TTG, they did it without my knowledge or consent. You got that?"

The fire in his blue eyes convinced her as much as the uncomfortable grip on her still sore chin.

"I've got it."

"You'd better," he said, the anger still hot. "Now, do you want to work the wedding arrangements yourself or not?"

"Not."

"Dammit all to hell! I'm past being civilized and modern and reasonable about this. If I have to lock you in those chains your cousin talked about and drag you to the altar, I will. One way or another, you're going to marry me."

"Oooooh."

Gina batted her eyes and thought about leading him on a little longer. She decided against it, primarily because she wasn't quite sure he wouldn't follow through with that bit about the chains.

"As much as I might enjoy the kinky aspects of your proposal," she breathed, "I think we should go for something a little more traditional."

"Then for God's sake," he bellowed, "tell me what the hell you want."

Whoa! What happened to the smooth, polished diplomat who'd seduced her with his charm and sophisticated wit? This glimpse of the angry male under Jack's urbane shell thrilled and made her just a tad nervous. Yielding to the age-old feminine instinct to soothe and soften and placate her mate, Gina stroked his cheek.

"What I want," she said, "is for us to get off the bathroom floor. Then we'll make a call to your mom and get her up here on the next flight. After which, we'll haul ass to a lab and have our blood drawn so we can stand up before the nearest justice of the peace."

Jack agreed with the last portion of her agenda, if not the first. Instead of pushing to his feet and pulling her up with him, he kept her anchored to the fluffy bath mat. The fire went out of his eyes, the irritation out of his voice.

"Are you sure that's what you want?" he asked in a much subdued tone.

"That's what I want."

"No big fancy wedding? No exotic theme?"

"No big fancy wedding." With silent apologies to Nikki and Samuel and Kallie, she lied her heart out. "No exotic theme. Just you and me and our immediate families in front of a JP."

* * *

Gina should have known that plan wouldn't hold up against the combined assault of her sister, her grandmother and Jack's mom, Ellen. All right, maybe she didn't really want it to. She'd given too much of herself and her energy to the party-planning business. In her heart of hearts, she secretly wished for at least a little splash.

Still, she had to work to overcome her irritation when her boss called less than an hour after Gina and Jack had emerged from the bathroom and announced their intentions to the assembled entourage. Vickers, Gina thought immediately. The little toad probably had TTG on his speed dial.

"Gina," Nikki gushed in her rapid-fire way, "I just heard! You've finally come to your senses."

"I…"

"I'm so, so glad you've agreed to marry your sexy ambassador."

"I have, but…"

"Listen, kiddo, I know Jack is hot to get you to the altar before you change your mind. I also know you want to keep the wedding small and intimate, but the midtown venue's available Thursday evening."

"Nikki…"

"My office, ten tomorrow morning. We'll hammer out the details. Oh, and bring your grandmother. I've been wanting to meet her since the day my father announced he was leaving my mother for her. God, I wish he had! Might have saved me thousands of dollars in shrink fees. *Ciao,* my darling. And don't worry. TTG will send you off in grand style."

Send you off in grand style.

The blithe promise had been intended to reassure. It acted instead like a bucket of frigid water. Every spark of Gina's newfound joy got a thorough dousing.

Grandmama, she thought on a wave of dismay. How could she move to D.C. and live with Jack? Not that he'd remain in

D.C. much longer. Vickers had hinted he was being considered for a major diplomatic posting. London was a definite possibility. So was Athens.

Heartsick, she caught Sarah's eye and telegraphed a silent signal. Her sister's hidden antenna were obviously in full receive mode. She nodded and moments later pushed through the swinging door to the kitchen. As soon as she saw Gina's face, concern clouded her green eyes.

"What's the matter?"

"Nothing out of the ordinary," Gina said bitterly. "I'm just being my usual, selfish self."

"Selfish how?"

"I didn't even think about Grandmama when I agreed to marry Jack. She's so looking forward to the baby. She's already talking about converting the study to a nursery. How can I just flit off and leave her alone?"

"She wants you to be happy. She wants both of us to be happy. You know she does."

Gina might have believed her if not for the guilt clouding Sarah's forest-green eyes. She'd experienced the same wrenching pangs before her wedding to Dev. They hadn't eased until Gina posed the possibility of moving back into the Dakota.

"Dev said he could set up a temporary headquarters here in New York," Sarah reminded her sister. "We could still do that. Or…"

The swish of the swinging door cut off whatever alternate Sarah had intended to propose. She and Gina both turned to face Zia.

"I'm sorry to intrude," she said. "But I wished to speak to you both, and this may be my only chance before Dom and I move to a hotel."

The heavy, stress-induced accent had disappeared. Zia was once again their gorgeous, self-assured cousin.

Or a third sister. One demanding to be included in this

girls-only enclave. The thought struck Gina all of two seconds before Zia gave it flesh and blood.

"As Gina knows," she said to Sarah, "I've just finished my last year of medical school at Semmelweis University in Budapest. It's a very prestigious institution and…well…"

She shrugged, as if to downplay what both sisters knew had to be a major accomplishment. "I've been offered a number of residencies in pediatric medicine," she continued after a moment. "One of them is at Kravis Children's Hospital. That's why I insisted on accompanying Dom on this visit. I…I have an interview with the head of the residency program tomorrow," she finished on a note of uncharacteristic hesitation.

"That's wonderful," Sarah said with unfeigned delight. "You and Grandmama will be able to visit and get to know each other better."

"Yes, well…" Zia's glance shifted from one sister to the other. "The duchess has invited me to live with her, should I do my three-year residency here in New York City. I'm overwhelmed by her generosity but I don't wish to impose on her. If the idea concerns you…either of you…or in any way makes you think I'm taking advantage of her, please tell me."

Gina wished she were a better person. She really did! Here she was, wracked with guilt one moment at the prospect of leaving her grandmother alone. In the next, she was battling a toxic niggle of jealousy at the idea of this ultra-smart, ultra-achieving woman taking her place in the duchess's heart.

And of course, because Zia *was* so damned smart, she read every emotion that flitted across Gina's face.

"I will not live here if you don't wish it," she said quietly. "Or you, Sarah. I know how much you love the duchess. How much she loves you. If it will cause you or her heartache, I'll turn down the offer from Kravis. None of you will ever hear from me again."

Gina knew the speech came straight from the heart. But it was the mist that sheened her cousin's dark eyes that obliterated any and every doubt. Somehow, someway, the knowledge that brilliant, self-assured Anastazia St. Sebastian was susceptible to human emotion made everything all right.

The jealousy fell away, leaving only a profound thankfulness. Smiling, she reached out and squeezed Zia's hand.

"I think it would be wonderful for Grandmama to have your company."

Sixteen

Nicole Tremayne came through as promised. TTG sent Gina and Jack off in grand style.

The balmy June evening was perfect for an outdoor ceremony. Thousands of tiny white lights gleamed in the topiary trees outlining the terrace of TTG's midtown venue. More lights sheathed in filmy white netting were hung in graceful loops to form an archway from the reception room to the dais. The platform itself was framed by antique wrought-iron. The intricate iron work was painted pearl-white and intertwined with netting, lights, ivy and fragrant yellow honeysuckle.

Gina and Jack had kept the guest list small. Relatively small, that is, compared to the hundreds who usually attended TTG's functions. Still, the attendees filled eight rows of white chairs arranged in a semicircle on the terrace overlooking the East River.

Gina's coworkers at TTG came as guests for a change instead of employees. Jerome and his wife had been invited, of course, and Maria beamed from her seat in the front row. Dominic sat beside her, his black eye still noticeable but considerably reduced in size and discoloration.

Jack's guests filled the seats on the other side of the aisle.

Following her son's wishes, Ellen had been ruthless. She'd axed every one of the political cronies her husband had tried to add to the list. Only Jack's family, close personal friends and associates survived the hatchet. In his case, though, "close" included the Secretary of State, the current U.S. Ambassador to the U.N. and Virginia's lieutenant governor.

"You ready, Gina?"

Kallie was the only of her fellow employees not seated out front. She'd volunteered to get the major players in place and cue the music. The wings in her red hair were yellow tonight in keeping with the yellow roses that wreathed the hair of the bride and her attendants.

The event coordinator in Gina had her taking a quick peek through the gauze curtains to make sure everyone was where they were supposed to be. Sure enough, Jack waited under the wrought-iron arch with his groomsmen. Dev stood tall and handsome beside him. Dale Vickers was arranged next to Dev. Gina grimaced inwardly but reminded herself of her resolution to *try* to build a better relationship with the little toad.

She let the curtain drop and sent a smile to the other three women clustered with her in the small anteroom. Her grandmother, regal in royal blue silk and lace, looked like the grand duchess she was. Gina had asked Zia to be one of her attendants. And Sarah, of course. They were each wearing the dress of her choice. Zia had hit the shops on 5th Avenue and found a body-hugging gold silk sheath that dipped to her waist in the back. With her black hair piled loosely on top of her head, the rear view was sure to drop most of the male jaws in the house when she glided down the aisle.

Sarah's dress was one of the retro classics she still favored despite Dev's repeated attempts to get her to buy out Rodeo Drive. This one was a Balenciaga that fell in soft, shimmering folds in the same vivid green hue as the Russian emerald Dev had slipped on her finger when they'd become engaged.

Gina's choice of rings was more traditional, if you could

call a three-carat marquise traditional. Particularly since Jack had upped the weight from her original choice and had the stone set in a band studded with another three carats of baguettes.

The diamonds' glitter didn't compare to the sparkle in Gina's smile as she gave Kallie the go-ahead. "I am so ready."

She wasn't sure, but she thought Sarah and the duchess let out a collective sigh of relief. Even Zia perked up as the music swelled and she led the way down the aisle. Sarah gave her sister a quick kiss and went next. Then Gina slipped her arm through her grandmother's.

As they made their slow progress under the arch of netting and tiny white lights, Gina couldn't believe how her world had changed so drastically in such a short time. Was it only two months since Grandmama had made this same, slow walk with Sarah? Two and a half months since Gina had peed on a little purple stick and felt her world tilt off its axis? Those frantic days might have happened in another life, to another person. Everything in Gina's world now was right and bright and perfect.

The duchess seemed to agree. When she and her youngest granddaughter reached the dais, her faded blue eyes shone with love. "My dearest Eugenia. I'm so very proud of you."

Gina wouldn't cry! She wouldn't! She wanted to, though. Big, fat, wet, sloppy tears that would streak her entire face with mascara.

Uh-oh! Jack must have sensed how close she was to a meltdown. He took a hasty step forward, smiling as he relieved the duchess of escort duty.

"I'll take it from here."

Bending, he dropped a kiss on his soon-to-be-grandmother-in-law's cheek. She murmured something for his ears only. Probably the same death threat she'd issued to Dev, Gina guessed, threatening him with unspeakable agony if he hurt so much as a single hair on her head.

Jack acknowledged the warning with a solemn nod. Then

his eyes were on Gina. Only on Gina. Her glorious smile, her tumble of silvery blond curls, her laughing blue eyes. He tucked her arm in his, amazed and humbled by the fact he'd been given the precious gift of love twice in one lifetime.

In all the excitement of the past week, he and Gina had almost missed their second appointment with their OB doc. They'd gone in yesterday and had the first ultrasound done. Jack carried a copy of the scan in his tux pocket now, right next to his heart. As far as his parents knew, he and Gina would welcome the Mason family's first set of twins.

First things first, though! Jack's number one priority at the moment was getting a wedding band on Gina St. Sebastian's finger. He practically dragged her into position on the dais and issued a swift instruction to the senior judge of the U.S. Court of Appeals for the Second Circuit, who also happened to be his former college roommate.

"Let's do this!"

Epilogue

What an exciting, frightening, wonderful week this has been! Eugenia, my darling Eugenia, finally admitted what I've known since the day she returned from Switzerland. She's in love, so very much in love, with the father of her babies. Babies! I can't wait to cradle them in my arms, as I once held Gina.

Then there's Sarah, my lovely Sarah. It makes my heart sing to see her so happy, too. I suspect it won't be long before she and Dev start their family, as well.

I thought my life's work would be complete when I escorted those two precious girls down the aisle. How odd, and how wonderful, that another young and vibrant twosome has helped fill the void of losing them. Dominic goes back to Hungary in a few days and is pressing me to return to my homeland for a visit. I shall have to think about that. In the meantime, I'll share Anastazia's trials and tribulations as she begins what I know will be a grueling residency.

Who would have imagined my plate would be so full at this late stage in my life?

From the diary of Charlotte,
Grand Duchess of Karlenburgh

* * * * *

If you loved Gina's story, don't miss her sister's tale,
A BUSINESS ENGAGEMENT
Available now from USA TODAY *bestselling author*
Merline Lovelace and Harlequin Desire!

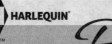

REQUEST YOUR FREE BOOKS!
2 FREE NOVELS PLUS 2 FREE GIFTS!

HARLEQUIN

Desire

ALWAYS POWERFUL, PASSIONATE AND PROVOCATIVE

YES! Please send me 2 FREE Harlequin Desire® novels and my 2 FREE gifts (gifts are worth about $10). After receiving them, if I don't wish to receive any more books, I can return the shipping statement marked "cancel." If I don't cancel, I will receive 6 brand-new novels every month and be billed just $4.55 per book in the U.S. or $4.99 per book in Canada. That's a savings of at least 13% off the cover price! It's quite a bargain! Shipping and handling is just 50¢ per book in the U.S. and 75¢ per book in Canada.* I understand that accepting the 2 free books and gifts places me under no obligation to buy anything. I can always return a shipment and cancel at any time. Even if I never buy another book, the two free books and gifts are mine to keep forever.

225/326 HDN F4ZC

Name _____ (PLEASE PRINT) _____

Address _____ Apt. # _____

City _____ State/Prov. _____ Zip/Postal Code _____

Signature (if under 18, a parent or guardian must sign)

Mail to the **Harlequin®** Reader Service:
IN U.S.A.: P.O. Box 1867, Buffalo, NY 14240-1867
IN CANADA: P.O. Box 609, Fort Erie, Ontario L2A 5X3

Want to try two free books from another line?
Call 1-800-873-8635 or visit www.ReaderService.com.

* Terms and prices subject to change without notice. Prices do not include applicable taxes. Sales tax applicable in N.Y. Canadian residents will be charged applicable taxes. Offer not valid in Quebec. This offer is limited to one order per household. Not valid for current subscribers to Harlequin Desire books. All orders subject to credit approval. Credit or debit balances in a customer's account(s) may be offset by any other outstanding balance owed by or to the customer. Please allow 4 to 6 weeks for delivery. Offer available while quantities last.

Your Privacy—The Harlequin® Reader Service is committed to protecting your privacy. Our Privacy Policy is available online at www.ReaderService.com or upon request from the Harlequin Reader Service.

We make a portion of our mailing list available to reputable third parties that offer products we believe may interest you. If you prefer that we not exchange your name with third parties, or if you wish to clarify or modify your communication preferences, please visit us at www.ReaderService.com/consumerchoice or write to us at Harlequin Reader Service Preference Service, P.O. Box 9062, Buffalo, NY 14269. Include your complete name and address.

HDI3R

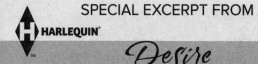
"**D**on't you ever get tired of acting?" Logan asked, his casual tone not matching the dangerous tension emanating from him.

"What do you mean?"

"The various roles you play to fool men into accepting whatever fantasy you want them to believe. One of these days someone is going to see past your flirtation to the truth," Logan warned, his voice a husky growl.

She arched her eyebrows. "Which is what?"

"That what you need isn't some tame lapdog."

"I don't?"

"No." Espresso eyes watched her with lazy confidence. "What you need is a man who will barge right past your defenses and drive you wild."

"Don't be ridiculous," she retorted, struggling to keep her eyes off his well-shaped lips and her mind from drifting into the daydream of being kissed silly by him.

"You can lie to yourself all you want," he said. "But don't bother lying to me."

It wasn't until he captured her fingers that she realized she'd flattened her palm against his rib cage. She tugged to free her hand, but he tightened his grip.

"Let me go."

"You started it."

She wasn't completely sure that was true. "What's gotten into you today?"

He smiled. "You know, I think this is the first time I've ever seen you lose your cool. I like it."

How had he turned the tables on her in such a short time?

"I'm really not interested in what you—"

She never had a chance to finish the thought. Before she guessed his intention, Logan lowered his lips to hers and cut off her denial. Slow and deliberate, his hot mouth moved across hers.

Scarlett wanted to cry out as she experienced the delicious pleasure of his broad chest crushing her breasts, but he'd stolen her breath. Then the sound of the doors opening reached them both at the same time. Logan broke the kiss. Eyes hard and unreadable, he scrutinized her face. Scarlett felt as exposed as if she'd stepped into her casino wearing only her underwear.

Breathless, she asked, "Did that feel like acting?"

Find out what happens next in
AT ODDS WITH THE HEIRESS
by Cat Schield

Available January 2014 from Harlequin® Desire.

Desire

ALWAYS POWERFUL, PASSIONATE AND PROVOCATIVE.

From *USA TODAY* bestselling author
Elizabeth Lane,
a novel that asks, can desire trump deception?

Haughty and handsome, ski resort owner
Wyatt Richardson has never met a problem
he couldn't buy his way out of. Facing the
unexpected custody of his teenage daughter
and her newborn son, he swiftly hires a nanny to
handle them both. His attraction to Leigh Foster
is an unexpected perk. He's confident the feeling
is mutual.

Leigh knows she is on shaky ground. Falling for
her new employer could prove devastating—
especially if Wyatt finds out her true connection
to baby Mikey. But when the billionaire's strong
arms beckon, will she be powerless to refuse?

Look for
THE NANNY'S SECRET
next month, from Harlequin Desire!

Wherever books and ebooks are sold.

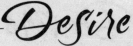